Day Trip
An Inspirational Adventure

by
Martin Evans

PublishAmerica

Baltimore

First printing

ISBN: 1-4137-1567-2
PUBLISHED BY PUBLISHAMERICA, LLLP
www.publishamerica.com
Baltimore

Printed in the United States of America

Dedication

This book is dedicated to my Dad, a man who in his own way taught me the meaning of courage. He also gave me the gift of never being able to complain.Thanks Dad. Your life and how you lived it has given me the inspiration to write this book

This book was first started in a newsroom in Gloucester during a lunch break, and was concluded on a cruise liner in the Caribbean Ocean between Panama and Columbia. Dreams do come true if you want them to.

It was a cold Thursday morning, the wind had a sharp bite and it was confused with sporadic diamonds of sleet that pierced the skin as it pounded from the heavens. I can remember the feeling, the skin on my arms tightening as it braced against the elements; I still get flashbacks to that morning when a goose bump appears on the surface of my arm like a mole trying to escape from frosty earth.

Looking back, this was probably a sign from the gods, as the two other people I met on that day were fairly religious. They weren't wearing dog collars or anything as obvious but one wore sandals, had a beard and was married to a woman named Mary. A peaceful man with a heart of gold, James was Eton educated and a trained chartered accountant. He had rebelled against the system and was a contented vegetarian, being happiest sleeping outside, gazing at the Milky Way and getting genuinely excited by seeing a shooting star pass through the Plough.

Sharon was a conventional nurse who worked for the NHS, but she did have psychic and holistic tendencies. She said that if she held her hands over someone's feet, a burning sensation would penetrate her soul and she could tell if any abnormalities existed in the person's body. She also believed she could heal them with her mind and could also see auras! Now if that doesn't count as religious then I don't know what does.

And of course there is me, just me. Not religious with no special powers and devoid of any healing ability, or at least that's what I thought.

The rain had cleared come ten o'clock and the skies were now clouded with grey cirrocumulus. I knew it was going to be one of those days, but I didn't realise what an effect it was going to have on my life.

We were scheduled to meet at eleven and I was over thirty minutes away so I increased the force on the acceleration pedal and headed for the forest. I had been there before, only once, but that was more than enough.

I was seven minutes late when I arrived at their dwellings. I am a stickler for punctuality so I apologised profusely. They looked at me strangely as they jumped in their mini-bus, which was a twenty-year-old converted ex-police van and headed off to do their final shop up for tea bags. They were halfway down the road before I had a chance to blink and take my first breath of fresh forest air.

I walked through the front door leaving my luggage neatly stacked by the side of the entrance. I could hardly fit through the large dining room as it was stacked floor to the ceiling with containers of toys and medical aid. Syringes were falling from split boxes and tins of food were rolling on the floor. At first sight it looked as if they had been burgled but their dog was contentedly tucked up in the corner on top of a pile of old newspapers. The bottom paper dated back exactly three years to the day. I did not realise it yet but the number three would play a significant role in the next three weeks and also on the rest of my life.

Time Stands Still for No Man!

The time was going like a racing driver on the last lap earlier in the day but now it appeared as if the engine had ceased on this performance vehicle. Each minute seemed like an eternity as I patiently waited in the slum for the organisers to come. Flies were hovering around a naked light bulb that was dangling from the ceiling and displaying more charisma than anyone in the building. I am sure a cockroach ran across the chair I was sitting on, but instead of a normal gut reaction of swatting it with one of the nearby papers, I just chuckled to myself as it obviously had a sense of urgency that I wished others would emulate. Frustration was starting to set in and I could feel it move from the temples on my head and down my spine. I was going in and out of consciousness, and my head would nod forwards from the boredom.

Suddenly the silence was broken by the screeching of tyres braking just outside the dump of a residence.

They were finally back and came pounding through the door, each carrying containers that were bulging at the sides. Stretch marks were visible on the big white recycled box that was formerly the packaging for economy toilet rolls. I chortled quietly as I reflected how the box resembled her physique. It was chocked full of Earl Grey breakfast tea bags, thick sliced bread and a few dozen boxes of high tar cigarettes.

The clock genuinely seemed to be struggling against going forward and creaked with every mulish mechanical movement. It obviously knew its owners at that time far better than I did.

Ready, Steady

Another hour went by with no activity before it was decided that we had better get a move on and it was another hour after this, at three o'clock when the wheels finally started to roll. They jumped in the truck, and tucked themselves up in their cosy cabin which was adorned with decorative features, fairy lights and numerous "I've been to flags." On the dash board in front of the steering wheel was a twelve-inch long porcelain horse with wooden carriage and little beer barrels. There were dozens of plastic toys that you get when you buy a child's meal at a burger bar, and the remnants of some of the tasty, high fat, higher cholesterol products in the gaps between the chairs. How they could see out of the window boggled me.

Sharon, James and I were bundled into makeshift seats screwed into the back of the van. She flopped out of her cosy seat in the front and slammed the sliding door shut with vicious ferocity before jumping back into her seat, which had been moulded over time to fit her ample rear.

There was not a lot of room in the back, which was formerly a portable cell. My feet were resting on a gas bottle with a travel cooker propped to the side. Long copper poles were poking from the back and would vibrate on the side of my face as the van chugged along. The suitcases were stacked just behind where we were sitting and a vanity case that was balanced on top of the pile would fall off and hit me at regular intervals.

To the left of me about a foot away was a tall square toolbox that I would lean on to rest when I got weary. The sharp edges of the cube made indentations on my skin and the blood vessels would rise where the object made contact. This was the most uncomfortable I had ever been in my life but I did not realise then how much I would appreciate the small confined space after the three weeks were up.

Snail's Pace

The whole journey was paced at no faster than fifty miles per hour in an attempt to stretch the fuel and obtain maximum efficiency. That was the main reason they gave, but I think their overt psychopathic side had another. Just from this alone, the normal hectic and fast pace of my life was being tied down like a wild horse being tamed. They were trying to control our lives from the outset and they would strive to condition each of us into their way of living. If the three of us did not have each other, we may have been tamed and changed.

There were two others with us in the van but they did not bond like the three of us did. One was called Taz. She was a fifteen-year-old-girl, traditionally gothic in appearance, who was experiencing family troubles at home. She came away to escape the strife and trauma for a few weeks but jumping from a play school to a war zone would make her appreciate exactly what she had left. She was obviously the most vulnerable in the group and the two of them knew this, and made her sit between them in the front.

The other was Andy. He was a seventy-year-old cowboy who could talk the hind legs off of a donkey and was full of useless facts that were of benefit to no one. He also had a stale smell that was a mixture of chewing tobacco and urine, as most people his age do! The chain-smoking did not help either. Andy had no teeth and when he talked his bottom lip and nose would almost touch.

There were others in the team as well. Following behind was a seven-ton truck that had been donated for the trip by a charity with religious connections. Emblazoned on the side in bright yellow paint was the wording "God loves you" and the dark blue vehicle became fondly known as the God mobile. In this Christian chariot was a family of six. They consisted of dad, Dave, who was driving with his two eldest sons along side him. He was a thirty-six-year-old fire-eater with a medium-length ponytail. His eldest was a quiet eleven-year-old boy who did very little wrong but always got the blame for everything. As he was the oldest he was normally left in charge of the others. His brother was nine years old and was the most intelligent of the four and also the tallest but would go into sulks if he didn't get his own way. In the box behind the cabin was a boarded area with a side door that the rest were made to travel in.

The mother, Gerri, was only twenty-nine and displayed immaturity at times but was quite maternal to her offspring. Her hair went down to the centre of her back and was bright ginger in colour. Her two bundles of joy were a five-year-old who was always attention seeking and a two-year-old who had his own way, full stop. Every hour of every day you could guarantee you would hear, "mum, mum, MUM," each one getting louder after the other and if a fourth "mum" was required, it would be combined with the stamping of feet and a loud whine.

Nearly There!

We were about ten miles from Dover when the trouble with the van started. A loud noise like a drum being banged could be heard emanating from the front left wheel. It was hardly surprising as the vehicle was bulging to the point that the sides had formed a convex outline, and of course, who was sitting above the wheel in question?

We managed to limp to a truck stop which I thought was aptly named and stopped, for six hours. We established that the brake pad had worn to the bare metal despite them telling us that they put the van in for full service only two days before. It had taken us over seven hours to almost make Dover. The normal average, mediocre, run of the mill man could do it in under three but after only 200 miles, three service station stops and four wrong turns we had already missed the boat, which was booked for eight o'clock, or so we were told.

Missing the Boat

The time was nearing ten at night and the temperature was starting to drop. The breakdown recovery had been called out and I was waiting rather impatiently. I did not want to spend my first night of a life changing mercy mission on British soil.

Eventually the recovery did turn up but it was a tow truck with no tools or spare parts. A greasy-haired man got out with a cigarette dangling from his bottom lip and food stains down the front of his blue, oversized overalls. He said that his instructions were to tow the van back to the Forest! It was bad enough not going forward let alone being told to go back. I felt like I was trapped in a giant game of snakes and ladders, and all the steps had been smothered in grease from the mechanics mullet.

It took over half an hour to persuade him that we did not want a lift but a repair job. I explained that I could have done the job myself if he could only get me a brake pad but a confused look embraced his face as it tilted to the side like a small dog not understanding a command. He reluctantly called his governor and told him what was needed before jumping back into his truck and driving off without even saying goodbye. The time was now going mercilessly slow but as the clock struck midnight another recovery vehicle could be seen coming from the distance like a hungry bird diving for it's prey.

A younger, clean shaven mechanic this time pulled up next to the disabled van. He wound down his window whilst pointing at the inoperative wheel. Shaking his head he asked if that was it.

A sigh of relief from his arrival was replaced with steam rising from my throat and jetting out of my ears when the mechanic realised he had the wrong size pad even before he got the tyre off. The whistling sound that I was transmitting could be heard for miles and sounded like a steam train running over a level crossing at high speed. This mechanic was far more competent than the first and drove off apologetically to get the right size. After a few more hours of hanging around twiddling our fingers, he heroically returned and the job was finally done. We were at long last making our way towards Dover.

He's Still Waiting and Hesitating

We were scheduled to meet the last member of our convoy at six o'clock in a lay-by just before the port.

The time was now three in the morning and Geoff was lingering agitatedly inside the cab of his thirty-eight foot long heavy goods vehicle. He had fretfully thumped his fingers on his steering wheel so many times that it had almost lost its circular shape. The normally placid flat cap wearing Yorkshire man had transformed into a pissed off hyperactive mutant like creature who gave the impression that he was about to explode. The ticking sound emanating from his shirt pocket did little to ease my apprehension of him detonating but when he pulled his travel clock out for the thousandth time in nearly ten hours I did feel slightly eased.

He had been waiting for hours and they did not even show him the courtesy of a phone call despite the fact that he had donated three weeks of his life, his lorry and his business. He was minutes away from turning around and driving home but the desire to do something positive had kept him for just a few more seconds.

I knew exactly how he was feeling because I had been kept hanging around for over an hour at the beginning of the day and that was bad enough, but this was nine times worse.

They told him that they couldn't get a signal from their mobile phone, despite many social calls to their friends about trivial things like taping their favourite television shows for them whilst they were away. They also said that they had tried many times from a public phone box at the service station but he was always engaged. More excuses were made, which had little effect, but Sharon and I spent twenty minutes calming him down and rationalising. Instead of more disingenuous apologies I told him how important he was to the trip and finally the convoy was rolling again.

I Smell Salt

Finally, after fifteen hours we had, at long, long last made the glorious sight that was Dover. It was a wonderful sensation seeing those beautiful white cliffs towering in front of us, the huge metal cranes dominating the skyline and of course the most reassuring sight of all, the ferries. By now I didn't expect everything to go smoothly and I was not disappointed. Because we missed our scheduled departure there would not be another ferry free until the morning, and the office that we had to obtain our green card international driving licence from was closed. This meant that for the next three weeks we would be driving illegally.

Most of the group got their heads down for the few hours that we had to wait but I was restless and there was no way I could get comfortable in the cell so I sat in one of the many waiting rooms. Luckily, before we left I decided to pack a variety of reading material. I dipped my hand into my backpack and pulled out at random a positive mental attitude book. It was certainly overdue and I needed a shot of positivism worse than a heroin addict needing a fix. I opened the book and the pages fell open at chapter three, which was entitled "Look for the Seed of an Equivalent Benefit." After reading the chapter for over an hour, I struggled to find the seed of my situation but after deep thought and consideration I realised that at least setting sail after six would mean we could see the sights and landscape going into France, which would not have been possible if we set sail at the planned eight o'clock in the evening.

I also looked around the room and saw lorry drivers who had been held up at customs for days and who had to live their entire lives on the road. This made me realise how cushy my life in general was.

I must have nodded off because I had just dived head first into a pool full of chocolate that was surrounded with blonde haired naked mermaids. I was just about to de-scale one of the bustier blondes when Sharon tapped me on the back and woke me with a jolt from my delightful dream. The melted chocolate from a bar of fruit and nut that I had been sucking on was dribbling from the side of my mouth and down my cheek. Why I had mermaids in my dream was beyond me at the time but looking back it could be because we were just about to be sea bound.

Sharon said that they were nearly ready to go and we should all get together. I picked my book up from the floor. Although it dropped from my hands when I fell asleep, it was still on the same page that I had left it on and I now always look for that seed in any negative situation.

We all bundled back into the variety of vehicles and joined the queue to board the ship. It was moving at a steady pace and feeling the change from hard tarmac beneath us to the rigid metal of the vessel was wonderful. As we left the British shore, I did not realise that by the time I was to set foot back onto our glorious country I would have looked for more than a seed, in fact it would have equated to a whole plantation.

The ferry eased away from the docks at precisely eight-thirty and I climbed the narrow stairway to the open deck. Everyone else headed straight for the restaurants and bars but I was glad to have my own space. The sun had just risen in the far horizon and its orange glow was mirrored on the surface of the sea. The bright coloured ripples against a dark blue background was a wonderfully calming image that replicated an oil painting that I had seen hanging in a posh restaurant in London. Memories started flooding back to my first girlfriend whom I had tried to impress by taking her there.

A fairly strong wind was blowing in a southerly direction and as I faced it I could not breathe from its mighty force. The seagulls caught my attention. They seemed to hover effortlessly in the breeze. Watching these birds was an immense learning experience. They had honed their flying skills to a fine art and I thought that if they could do that, why couldn't I? Not flying of course because that is anatomically impossible for humans, or is it? Practice makes perfect and they had motivated me to put more time into improving skills in my occupation and hobbies.

I was also jealous of the amount of freedom they had and suddenly felt sympathetic for my Nan's little blue-faced budgie that was cooped up in a two-foot tall cage, eating only what he was given, drinking only water and not being able to do anything but look at his reflection in a dusty, excrement covered mirror. Lots of thoughts were passing through my mind and the time seemed to fly faster than any seagull could imagine.

The constant blanket of blue had a green-coloured rip in the top right corner that kept getting bigger. I was still in a dreamy state when I realised that the tear was France. The small dot got larger and larger with every passing lap of water and suddenly it was on top of us like a big monster as the ferry backed into Calais.

I made my way down the small narrow stairs and bumped into the two of them. They were making their way back to the van and were loaded up with boxes of cigarettes, bottles of wine, spirits, perfumes, and bags of sweets. They must have spent at least two weeks of their giro and disability benefit on these luxuries. I thought it was terribly wrong for the hard-working, tax paying people of our proud nation to subsidise these antics while they were living literally like pigs in muck.

France at Last

We all gathered around the vehicles just as the doors to the ferry were opening, letting a ray of early morning sun light up the darkness of the interior of the vessel. Within minutes the convoy was rolling and heading straight for the first service station for a shower and to fill up with cheap petrol for the long journey that awaited us. The indicator was grazing the orange line on the fuel gauge when we arrived at Dover so there was an all round sigh of relief when the distinctive logo of the petrol station could be seen over the first hill.

We all scattered in different directions when we made the services. The kids headed straight for the numerous machines that are lined with cheap toys that you can win by lifting them with a mechanical claw that has all the strength of an underdeveloped French mosquito. Sharon and James strolled toward the picnic site that was an area of short cut lush green grass surrounded by tall oak trees. They had individually prepared their own packed lunch, which consisted of a cheese sandwich, an apple and a carton of orange juice. Their similar breakfasts were the first of many coincidences that the two and I would share. Taz practically flew like an eagle into the trees for a much-needed joint and Geoff walked to the café for a peaceful freshly cooked full English breakfast. He was joined by the parents and the noisy two who took delight in ordering a waitress in this self-service café. Andy went to the cigarette machine for a packet of the cheaper brand as he was down to his last five cartons.

I went to the toilets for a shower before joining Sharon and James in the quietness of the picnic area. I was shocked to see some bloke standing outside the convenience behind a table with a dish of money. He was thanking everyone as they walked out and calmly placed cash on his plate. I thought that this was rather strange as he did not look like a beggar, in fact he was wearing designer clothing, and I could not see a guitar hanging around in case he was a busker.

I would later learn that it was conventional to pay for using this convenience in most of the European countries that we would visit. I do not mind paying to satisfy some of my physiological needs such as the needs to eat and even reproduce, but paying to excrete! I had a shiny silver five pence piece lying at the bottom of my pocket so I relieved myself in their ultra clean units and dropped it in the half full dish on the way out. It made a nice clanging sound and mixed in nicely with the francs. I thought I had got away with my scam as I made my exit but the Frenchman started ranting in what seemed to be laced with European profanity. I could not understand a word of what he was blabbering but I calmly walked away as his blood vessels rose to the surface of his cheeks.

As I lay on the grass with James and Sharon I thought about the prospect of spending all of my currency that I had yet to purchase on urinating. Then my mind wandered to crouching behind a tree in the dead of night when everyone else had gone to sleep in order to save some hard-earned cash. Just before leaving, I popped to the petrol station shop for a bottle of freshly squeezed orange juice to keep me lubricated until the next of many stops. I only had English pounds on me because I forgot to change it to Euros on the boat.

A large rotund man was serving behind the counter and he was wearing a thin medium-sized red coloured T-shirt. He was definitely an extra large if not triple XL and the bottom of the shirt didn't even cover his navel. Stretch marks were visible from the front and that was bad enough, but worse still was his exposed posterior when he turned around and bent down to pick up some change that had fallen on the floor. A fat lady standing in the queue in front of me was obviously sexually excited at this extreme sight but it made me feel physically sick and almost put me off my juice. I placed my drink and a ten-pound note on the counter and he mumbled something under his breath, looked at a grubby laminated sheet under his desk and after a few calculations gave me my juice and my change in francs. It looked like a lot but when I counted it, I realised that I had been done. I went back and questioned the lack of change but he shrugged his shoulders and grunted.

A rather attractive brunette who was stacking shelves came over and asked if she could help. She had a pretty face with a roman nose and spoke reasonably good English. It was quite a sexy accent that made the hairs on the back of my neck tingle. She got out the laminated chart that was under the desk and explained that the change was correct but their exchange rate and their charge was very high. I looked at it and thought it was extortionate. I told James as he was involved in the world of finance and he advised me to never go to a place like that to exchange money, but to always look for a bank or reputable dealer and shop around for the best rate. I thanked him for his advice and put the small amount of change that I had left in a plastic pot that once held the film for my camera.

One Goes by the Wayside

We had been at this service station for over an hour and a half and I was getting rather restless so I went to the café where they were all munching away quite happily, all that is except for Andy. He was breathing rather heavily, walking from the van to the café, taking large strides and looking very unhappy. His bottom lip was unromantically caressing his nostrils and the corners of his mouth were drooping below his chin in what appeared to be a World record girning attempt. I asked him what was wrong and he told me that he had a burning sensation in his chest and he needed his pills, which were locked in the van, and the two would not open it up for him. I could not believe this and thought it was a joke; he then dragged his feet over to a large rock at the car parks exit, scuffing his shoes on the gravel all the way. Andy was really down with his head hung into the palm of his hands and he looked like a garden gnome sitting on a rockery, only needing a fishing rod in his hands and a red floppy hat to really look the part. He said that he had had enough and that he was going home.

I personally did not take him seriously but as the entourage made their way out of the building towards the car park Andy jumped up and darted to the van. When they unlocked the door,he bolted in, took his pills and then grabbed his two bags and small old-fashioned suitcase and calmly walked back to the rock he was previously sitting on. He got his mobile phone out, made a few calls and then slumped back into his original position. I thought he was joking about leaving, and that his performance was a play for attention. Geoff went over and knelt down besides him so their eyes met at the same level. He was talking very calmly and reassuring him.

Is It a Bird? Is It a Plane? No, It's a Taxi!

I could see all this from afar as I was sitting behind the wheel in the God mobile getting ready for my first stint of continental driving. In the distance, I could see a bright yellow-coloured taxi getting closer and it pulled up next to where Andy was sitting. He shot up, grabbed his bags and threw them with ferocity into the cab before jumping in. He slammed the door and off he went. Everybody sat in stunned silence at his actions because he was one of the keenest members of the group but looking back he probably did the right thing.

After a few more minutes, Andy was forgotten and the only talking point was getting back on to the road and how far we were going to get today. It was pointed out by Geoff that we needed to get as far as we could because there was a weekend driving ban on all vehicles over seven and a half tons in most of the continental European countries. It was now midday on Friday which meant we had less than twenty-four hours to drive 1,500 miles or we would have to stop for the weekend. The two said that they had no idea of this rule despite the fact that they did the trip last year. I suggested that we had better make a start or we would be stopping here over the weekend.

Dave was getting tired because he had driven all the way from England and his two restless children had been playing up so I volunteered to drive the God mobile. It took a huge amount of bravery to even contemplate such a task as the holy lorry was quite literally falling apart. It had dozens of rusted perforations all over the bodywork, large plates soldered into a jigsaw pattern and it also squeaked with every movement.

It was my first time behind the wheel on the trip, my first time ever driving a lorry and I was a virgin when it came to driving on the right hand side of the road.

I love new experiences, it's one of the ways that you learn in life, and this was certainly that. The steering was very strange. You could turn the wheel about 40 degrees and the lorry still would not turn. The gear stick had to be moved with immense force. After much heaving, it would crunch into place. The acceleration was abysmal. Dave gave me a useful piece of advice which was stay on the white line. If the driver's side wheel was on the white line then there would be plenty of room for lorries to pass in the overtaking lane. Well, that's the theory anyway!

I had been driving "in the cradle" which is truckers' terminology for being in the middle. The van was "taking the lead" and Geoff's juggernaught was "keeping eyeball." I had all of these types of lorry drivers jargon and paraphernalia thrown at me with reckless abandon on the CB as he wanted everyone to know that he used to be a professional long distance lorry driver before becoming a professional dosser. He kept telling me at regular intervals to stay on the white line. He said I kept deviating from the line and that I was putting the person on the passenger side at risk. This was nonsense as I kept to within three inches of the damn line all the time, but he wanted me to know who was boss.

While all of this was going on, she was in the van in front bending her body so that her head would lean across Taz and end up in his lap in a rather sexually suggestive position every time the van veered to the right. When it went to the left, she would shift her over ample sized butt so it squeezed Taz between them and would lean out of the window. She also ordered everyone in the van to do the same. It was a hilarious sight and she justified her orders by saying that it helped the van to steer and eased the suspension!

Another Stop

We had been driving for just over an hour when they indicated to the right. The information came across the CB that he needed to use the toilet and it would just be a quick stop. Through the windows on the back doors of the van and over the luggage I could see the top of the five occupants uniformly leaning to the right like penguins waddling in the snow as the van turned into the service station. We were all following the lead so the rest of the convoy also turned off and pulled up in the truck stop.

Dave got out of the lead van and opened up the bolted side door of the God mobile. His wife and kids limped out, obviously as distraught as a cluster of battery hens that had been violently shaken but the kids made the most of the stop and went for a quick leak. Everyone else just waited as it was only supposed to be a quick stop but as the watch showed twenty-five minutes had passed I started to get concerned.

My mind is active at the best of times but when I have nothing to do but wait it literally goes into overdrive and my conscious mind dances the tango with its subconscious next-door neighbour. I had all sorts of visions flashing through my mind from her attacking him with her snakelike tongue to him being abducted by a giant rat and sucked down the continental toilet pan. I was quite enjoying my visions when Sharon tapped on the window of the God mobile and said that we had been at this roadside pull-in for over forty minutes.

Suddenly in the distance I could see the two coming out of the revolving doors as they made their exit and were carrying three or four bags each of shopping and souvenirs. They said that they had a quick coffee whilst they were there. I could hardly believe it. They had kept us waiting for nearly an hour. Time was precious and they were both so blasé. My mind went back just a few heartbeats to the first day and how we were kept waiting for what seemed an eternity.

"Wagons rolling!" came screeching over the CB as he was now ready to depart and I could hardly wait.

I wanted to get at least 400 miles under my belt before I could relax for the evening. I had not slept for the entire duration of this adventure and I did not sleep too well the night before the trip as I was genuinely excited about the unknown that lay ahead. The goal of getting to bed after a hard day on the road was now my short-term goal. A goal is simply a dream with a date on it.

I have my ultimate long-term lifelong dream tattooed in my mind in irremovable, irrevocable, indelible ink and I read it at least ten times every day. I also have short-term goals which need to be achieved along the road to my personal self-actualisation, and of course I have my daily goals to help me get safely through the day. Getting to a nice cosy bed by midnight was today's. I'd recommend everyone to set themselves dreams and achievable goals because without a dream, how are you going to have a dream come true?! You very rarely get into your car not knowing where you want to go, and you even keep a map with you to keep you on course. Yet most people go through life not knowing where they want to go or what they want to achieve, which is a real shame.

Six hours, three coffee breaks and 150 miles later, it was decided that it was best if we found somewhere to stop for the night. I was starting to feel a bit wiry so agreed on the good old CB. I could tell they were about to pull in as everyone in the van started leaning to the right in domino effect from the front to the back. I thought they had made a mistake, as it was just a gravelled lay-by with a dingy unisex toilet. The grass verge was overgrown and there were no other vehicles. The convoy stopped and as she got out of the lead van the suspension valves breathed a sigh of relief. She clanked the handle on the side door with her masculine hands and got the bulbous blue gas bottle and travel cooker out from under James' bare feet.

The lay-by was illuminated when the match made contact with the gas and within minutes the kettle could be heard bubbling. I still thought that this was one of the many short stops until she said that she'd be sleeping in the back where the luggage was, on a large double quilt with fluffy pillows. She then questioned where everyone else would sleep. Here? I questioned to myself, not here in the middle of nowhere next to a busy motorway and by a smelly toilet, that if it could talk would say nothing but profanity.

Whilst I was disillusioned by the whole concept, it seemed that everyone else had accepted it and was finding a place to bed down. They took the back of the van, which was quite cushy because there was room to stretch out. They put the entire pile of luggage to the side and almost made a hotel room in the back. James made his bed on one of the seats in the van and rested his head on the toolbox. Sharon curled up on the other seat in front of James with her coat pulled over her arms for warmth and Taz sprawled over the driver's seat with her bum humped over the hand brake and her feet pressed against the passenger side window. The family took the God mobile and Geoff had the luxury of a cab that was more of a home to him than a shell is to a snail. There was only one place left to sleep and that was the great outdoors.

It was the first time that I had ever ventured into the deep, dark outside to sleep in my life, I had not even been in a caravan or tent so I jumped feet first into the proverbial deep end and I thrust myself straight into the sharp elements and the unknown of being under the stars. I got as far away from the pungent aroma emanating from the toilets as possible and nestled down under the greasy rear axle of Geoff's trailer. The large dirt and tar laden rubber tyres either side of me were my bedroom walls, the hard and bumpy tarmac road was my mattress and the underside of the dusty, oily, pipe ridden deck acted as my ceiling. As I huddled in my sleeping blanket fully clothed and tried my best to get to sleep, thousands of small stones and pebbles kept poking through my mantle, and with every shift of my body new stones would attach and embed themselves into my clothes. This kept me awake most of the time but on the rare occasions that I did drift off the cars zooming past only a few metres away would wake me. After three or four hours I had gone into survival mode and conditioned my mind to accept and even like the sound of the hum being generated by the speeding vehicles. I now find it rather relaxing and when I unwind and meditate I will normally put on a hairdryer to replicate the constant sound.

After a night on the tarmac and a few hours of uncomfortable sleep I was awoken by a bright ray of sunshine poking over a hill in the distance. It was reflected off the side mirror of the van parked behind and dazzled me with its intense luminosity. I slowly rose and stood up steadily as pain racked through my body. My back was aching, my shoulder blades were uncomfortably sore and my arms were ready to drop. Three more lorries and a car had also pulled into the lay-by. The cabs in the lorries were all curtained off and the windows to the car were steamed up, except for a few feet shaped transparent imprints. As I turned around I could see two rats squabbling over a piece of stale cheese in the grass verge to the side of me. I found this mildly amusing and quite entertaining, until a busty blonde with a skirt so short that it looked like a belt got out of the steamed up car, threw her handbag over her shoulder, put her lipstick thickly on and then wandered off down the road into the distance. I watched her from behind as she wiggled down the busy highway swaying her hips and winking her eye at every car and lorry that went past. Her eyeballs must have been really sore from all that eye lid movement and I'm sure other parts of her were sore from her professional activities as well. She got smaller and smaller the further away she went but the wiggle was still visible for miles.

The view of that gorgeous but somewhat sleazy posterior had turned into a dot on the landscape when the side door to the van slowly creaked open and Sharon slumped out. Within minutes the rest of the crew followed and everyone started to stretch. It was like a scene out of an early eighties breakfast show with mad Lizzy.

After two coffees and a wash down with a damp cloth we were all ready to go, all except for the two. They were quite happy lazing all day in the back of the van with a packet of fags and another cup of coffee. They had the keys to the ignition, so everything was in their hands and we did not know them too well at this stage so we all amused ourselves as best as anyone could at the side of a French road. I had woken at just gone six and it was now rapidly approaching eleven. The two snobbishly walked from the back of the van, each with a smouldering cigarette dangling from their lips and he jumped into the driver's seat. She stood by the side door with one hand on her hip and the other signalling everyone into the van, as they were ready to go. She was telling everyone to get a move on and her body language was showing signs of impatience, which was as hypocritical as you could get.

I have always practised adopting a positive body language that communicates to people that I'm confident but approachable and if she wanted to be considered a leader then it's something that she should have learnt. It's easy and it doesn't require any energy and ultimately pays off. Something as simple as standing tall with your shoulders back and head held upright gives an aura of authority without the need for a verbal backup.

The door was again slammed and she jumped into the passenger seat that was covered with a leopard skin cloth and the newly acquired wooden beaded seat cover that went out of fashion in the U.K. in the late eighties.

The Next Goal

Our next goal was reaching Austria by nightfall and a long journey was ahead of us. After travelling for what seemed a lifetime, we finally started seeing the welcome signs for the Austrian border, which was far more exciting than seeing Christmas lights going up and going past each signpost was like counting down to a new year. This came as a great relief as it demonstrated that progress was being made and at least we were getting closer to Romania.

When the ten kilometre indication could be seen on the tall green sign we were told by the knowledgeable two in the front to get our passports out ready for customs. James and I looked at each other quizzically and Sharon tried to explain that Austria was now part of the European Union. We would not need passports or identification to get through and she doubted that there would even be any manned presence on the border. The two then started muttering to each other before lighting another fag. As the convoy breezed through the unmanned and almost derelict border she said that we were lucky not to be delayed and the guards must be on their break. All this despite the fact that the booths in-between the roads were falling apart and had moss growing over them.

Another Country!

A few seconds later and we had finally made Austria and this felt like a major achievement. We'd been told on our first meeting that the voyage from start to finish would take three days and we had been travelling for more than that and we were not even half way there yet. Apparently we had covered about 850 miles of the 2,000 needed to get to Romania and we had less than three hours before we would have to stop for the weekend due to the travel restrictions. With time ticking away and tempo being against us, I thought that our leaders would be anxious to get us as far as conceivable but consternation bled through my body like an axe man running in a horror movie. I realised that a service station could be seen on the horizon and his hand was twitching over the gear stick. I thought that I must have been getting psychic tendencies as I predicted they would turn off. Less than sixty seconds later, they started swaying to the right and lived up to my premonition.

Over an hour later and after "just one more coffee" we were setting off again. Sitting in my irritating little seat, my mind wandered back. I had time to look around the shop six times whilst I was there and for the first time I was not complaining.

Serving hotdogs in the café to the side of the shop was one of the most beautiful, curvaceous and shapely women that I have ever seen. Despite her perfect figure, she did not smile once but as I found out going through the country Austrians do not smile and as a rule are devoid of a sense of humour. Notwithstanding her insufficiency of humour, I would have still liked to have a short-term relationship with her as I found her scowl rather sexy. If nothing else the erotic image helped to pass away the time as we headed towards Germany.

Is That Cheese?

It was the early hours of the morning when we next stopped and the convoy had driven for hours illegally. Physical exhaustion had forced us to pull over and that was just the passengers who had to put up with the two of them, not the drivers! This time the stop was a dingy little hut, poorly lit and in the middle of nowhere, although its small car park was full to the brim with trucks from all nations. I wondered why it was such a popular location and reasoned that it must be because the food was of a good standard, as I know truckers like their comestibles. We were all ushered in like sheep being rounded into a pen. Even the children were now ratty and irritable, which was understandable at two o'clock in the morning.

The family and the two settled round a large table and ordered a meal while Sharon, James, Taz and I sat on tall stools surrounding the counter. We all ordered fruit juices except the impressionable youngster who ordered vodka. I think she liked to drink alcohol in front of people as it made her feel grown up.

Behind the counter was a large illuminated menu that displayed the range of sausages that they offered. I felt a bit peckish so I conferred with my friends as to which of the sausages I should have. They had long and emaciated, short and corpulent, seasoned and spicy and a whole host of colours. After much deliberation, I decided on a large pork one which came complete with a fresh roll.

When I placed my order the elderly lady serving coughed in her hand then grabbed a sausage from a draw and placed it in what looked to be an industrial press. It was sizzling away as she snatched a bread roll from under a transparent dish on the counter and put it on a paper plate. As the roll made contact with the plate it sounded like a hammer being knocked onto wood and I doubted its freshness. She opened the grill and flipped the sausage with her fingers before quickly withdrawing and blowing and spitting on her digits, which she'd obviously burnt. After a few more seconds it was done and she again handled the meat with her fingers and dumped it onto the plate along side the roll and squeezed a dollop of mustard to the side before presenting me with the delicacy.

I cut into the roll with a blunt plastic knife. It was far from fresh but passable. The sausage did look particularly palatable, as it appeared to have large chunks of cheese placed intrinsically within. I carved the length of the delicacy and the juices flowed out. The centre of the sausage looked raw as it was a deep red colour and cold but the outside was hissing with the heat. I cut a small slice and passed it into my mouth. As I started to masticate I had a tingling sensation on my tongue and my taste buds went into overdrive.

After chewing for a few minutes I realised that it was not laced with nuggets of cheese, but chunks of fat. The look on James and Sharon's faces was incomprehensible as they both realised it was fat at the same time. Their expressions were identically horrified at the grisly sight, but I was hungry and it tasted acceptable so I carried on, saliva dripping from my mouth as I munched away. James was disgusted at this blatant carnivorous act with fat and grease oozing everywhere, but was more shocked when I asked for some butter for the roll which I duly slapped on.

My sausage was the main talking point for the rest of the evening and a source of great amusement. That fun and merriment was sharply broken when our leaders pills started to wear off and they began to get aggressive.

It all started quite stupidly. She put some money into a coffee machine and the coffee was not dispensed. She then started pulling all the knobs, pressing all the buttons and kicking the machine in an attempt to obtain her drink. When she had no joy she ran away like a spoilt child who had just been told off. She shouted at him so he tried to make the machine work. When it wouldn't, he started shouting at the poor assistant who was in her late sixties. Within minutes tempers were frayed and everyone was shouting at everyone else and chaos ensued. Seconds later, with her facial features uglier than normal, she stormed out stomping her feet as she made her dramatic exit, fleeing to the van.

The rain was pounding down with force as we left about half an hour later, the downpour corresponding to the mood of the latter part of the evening. We were all soaked from head to toe even though the van was parked just a few meters from the exit. Once inside everyone took the positions that they had adopted the previous evening. Taz was again in the front, the two were stretched out under a mattress in the back and Sharon and James claimed the small plastic-covered seats. I am no pansy but the concept of slumbering outside with persistent precipitation did nothing for me so I opted to make my bed on the floor of the automobile between the seats that slept James and Sharon. I had to curl up like a snake so that my body twisted around all of the many obstacles. The portable cooker doubled as a pillow and my contorted body ached with the hardness of the floor and made me appreciate the benefits of the now forgiving tarmac.

It was impossible to sleep so I just let my mind go into survival mode and visualised wandering through a beautiful park with fresh flowers and tall green-leafed trees. This technique, taught to me by a relaxation specialist, was working fine. I could feel the gentle breeze in the air and the soft, lush grass beneath me. I could hear the sounds of birds tweeting in the trees and could smell the flowers. That is until James' foot, which had not been washed for three days, fell of the edge of the seat and waffled me on the nose. Suddenly the conceived scent from the blooms was drastically replaced with the very real putrescent emanation of rotting skin.

After a sleepless night and two coffees for breakfast, we were illegally making our way towards Germany at the steady pace of fifty miles per hour and subsequently passed through the border. Not only did I find that the majority of Austrians are miserable but their enforcement services are also very lapse.

Deutschland Here We Come

We were in Germany for less than thirty minutes when loud piercing sirens started wailing and blue lights began to flash. The two in the front started to fluster and perspiration could be seen developing on their respective foreheads. The whole convoy duly pulled over. He said that everyone should stay in the van, not get out and not say anything. He then proceeded to jump out of his cab and waddled towards the policeman who was headed towards him. I could see him clearly in the mirror and I was sure that he had excreted in his underwear from the way he was walking. His greasy hair was dangling out of the back of his green coloured cap, which he hardly ever took off and his white sport socks were rolled down on his thin little ankles.

The oncoming police patrol officer was a dominating sight. Clad in a smart black uniform, standing at over six foot and wearing a belt that had a virtual office suspended from it. There were two sets of handcuffs, a notepad, phone, radio, truncheon, C spray, and a threatening pistol. He also had a cool appearance wearing shades, long leather boots, and chewing gum.

Our leader was flapping and looking quite dishevelled as the policeman calmly stood there with his arms folded looking down at him. He kept pointing to the vehicles and repeatedly said "humanitarian". He was rambling with little sense and was running out of breath when Geoff strolled over and told him to go back to the van and let him take care of it. After calmly debating our cause, he said that we were lucky not to be fined but we must pull off at the next available stop until one o'clock on Monday morning. The police escorted us to the next available services before zooming off down the motorway.

Hell in a Cell

It was almost poetic, or do I mean pathetic! For the next thirty-three hours we would be confined like convicted criminals in a former mobile cell, which was encapsulated in another zoned off area as we were prohibited from leaving the car park. It was almost like a bubble in a bubble that I wished would only pop. I thought about all the things in life that I wish I could burst with an ultra sharp, metal clad toothpick. One of which would be my stomach. I then realised that I did have the pointed, potentially painful instrument, and it was called "responsibility for my own life." I didn't need to wish I could pop my belly; I just needed to take control, exercise regularly and eat sensibly, without blaming others for my circumstances.

What on earth could we possibly achieve in all that time with nothing to do apart from make things to do? There is always something possible to help you towards your goal, such as reading a book, talking to people who are where you want to be or even some positive visualisations. There was no one around suitable to talk to so I was just about to jump into my imaginary leather clad black Porsche with personal number plate and take a quick ride down to the yacht when Sharon asked me if I would like a foot massage. I leapt at the chance of testing her "psychic abilities."

We both went to a quiet shaded area, which was a large traffic island and sat under a tree. I settled down on the dry short cut grass and removed my shoes and socks. Sharon knelt at the base of my outstretched legs and started humming. She then closed her eyes and went into a trance-like state, gently swaying at first and then erratically moving from side to side before hovering her hands over my feet and taking short sharp intakes of breath. This was no ordinary sight and I'm sure that if she were treating a diminutive old lady she would have terrified her to the point that she would saturate her economy style stay dry pads! I relaxed into the situation and Sharon started to rub my feet with gentle strokes.

As her fingers ran over each part of my foot she would tell me which part of the body it responded to. After a thorough rubdown, I was feeling invigorated and refreshed, that is until I was told about the numerous problems in my body and all the things that I would have to do to remedy them. After this semi-delightful hour of pleasure, it was time for yet another twiddle of the fingers before going down to the café for some food.

The atmosphere was apathetic and lifeless so I thought that I would make the best of a bad situation and start a mini-cabaret. Sharon, Geoff, Taz and James seemed to be delighted with the entertainment and the children came to life from their statue-like slumped positions, but the rest of the group thought I was being fatuous and every German in attendance thought that I was insulting them. After a good old sing song and a few Cilla Black impressions, it was time to retire to the van for a night of trying to sleep. It was bad enough being cramped in there lying tortuously on the floor, but to make matters worse they had parked as close to the motorway as they could when they had three acres of land to choose from.

I don't know where the night went but the sun was rising like freshly baked bread with a golden-coloured top. My body was now acclimatising to the conditions as I managed to get a few more hours sleep, but total exhaustion did assist in me being able to rest. I went for a walk around the complex wondering what on earth I was doing here. I left a lot behind and made a number of sacrifices to go on this mission and I was not getting anything out of it, and it was only day three. The boredom carried on for another twenty hours and in that time I managed to eat seven plates of chips. The reason for this was because it was the most reasonably priced dish on the exorbitantly priced menu. I regretted eating the deep-fried delicacy as it was counter productive to my goal of being slim, so I re-evaluated my goal and asked myself if I really wanted it. When the answer was yes I decided not to eat chips in moderation anymore.

The family must have spent over 200 pounds on food and our leaders probably spent more than that on their lavish lifestyle. Most of the comestibles they ordered they wasted. I could not believe it, I only ordered chips because I resented paying over the top and not only did I make sure I ate every single chip to get the best value for my mark, I also covered the meal with the contents of the free packets of condiments. The tomato sauce and mayonnaise improved the taste of the meal but the horseradish and mint relish combination left a lot to be desired.

Finally, after hours of waiting around and positive visualising until I could actually smell the leather of the Porsche; and even my high level of patience being tested to the maximum, we were ready to go. Which was fortunate, as I could not eat another chip. The restriction was lifted at six in the morning and we could have departed then but the two said they needed a shower and breakfast before they left and of course another coffee.

At six minutes past eleven the wheels on the bus were actually going round and round. The rubber from the tyres finally caressed the autobahn and we were at least one inch closer to our destination. That is until over an hour later when we started seeing signs for the region in Austria that we left two days ago. A hurried and confused look came over our leader's face as he swerved violently off the passage and did a u-turn saying that he had to go this way as he'd heard that their were major road works the other way and despite being hundreds of miles off course he had actually saved us hours!

As we meandered our way across Europe I went into one of my daydreams. I thought how this trip was akin to a winding river. A river can never run in a straight line as its force will always hit a weak piece of earth and erode that area. Then I likened the journey and the river with our leader, they were all bent!

As we travelled along the German Autobahn, I kept thinking that we were going round in circles as we consistently passed a sign saying Ausfart. I asked what this was as we has passed the same sign over fifteen times and she said that it was the capital of Germany and it was such a big place that was the reason for the many ways to get there. He said that it could not be as Frankfurter was the capital of Germany but he did concede that it must be a very large city. Sharon, who was multi-lingual awoke from a nap and looked at them in sheer disbelief. She pointed out that Frankfurter was a sausage and not a city and that anyone with an ounce of grey matter in their skull knows that Ausfart translates to exit. She pointed out that it was obvious even to the layman who did not understand the German language as it was posted at every egress.

Time was passing by like a flash of light but the experience was dragging with the equivalent passion of a stubborn, ill-fed mule. I don't quite know how but as we left Germany we managed to slice the side of Austria again for the second time before making our way to the Hungarian border. If a trained navigator would have charted our journey so far, I swear it would have looked like the work of a six-month-old hyperactive child with a melted crayon.

Hungry in Hungary

The Hungarian border was a totally different experience to anything that had been thrown at us to date. I was expecting to breeze through the periphery even though Hungary was not part of Europe. I should have learnt by now not to expect anything too positive on this trip, let alone everything going to plan. After this experience, I would be more erudite.

We made our way through the turnstiles and were told to pull in at the lorry park. All of the drivers got out of their respective vehicles with their customs papers and relevant items and headed for the large grey building that housed the custom officials. It was a menacing looking building, very plain in design and dismal in colour. I had bad vibes as soon as I saw the building and my instincts are normally very reliable. We were strictly told by the two that under no circumstances were we to leave the vehicles, not to set so much as a foot out of the door as you had to have special papers to walk around the border. They also said that if you did not have the required paperwork and you were seen wandering about you would be shot!

We were marooned in the van for over two hours. We had ran out of conversational topics and I could not stand another game of I-spy. My legs were starting to seize and I yearned for one of life's simple pleasures that the free man takes for granted: a walk in the open. All of a sudden the cow in the front had transformed into a horse and jumped up neighing. She said that she was going to find out what was going on as her teeth took on an equine appearance. Sharon queried her decision stating that she did not have the required documents and she herself had told us that we could not leave the van. Her response was that that was an hour ago and she had a special pass. She waddled towards the big grey building looking like a pregnant penguin from behind. We were supposed to be here for only a few minutes and over six hours had now passed.

The horse-faced penguin came back out, running her fingers through her hair with anxiety in her facial features and stress visible in her tensed fingers. She said that all Hungarians were bastards and Hungarian customs officials were even bigger twats. She was threatening to get on to the English Embassy and she also gibbered that they really did not know with whom they were messing. Within seconds he came stomping out revealing that he had waited for hours, gave his papers in and was then told to go to the back of the file. He clamoured that the person who brought the God mobile over six weeks ago must have really pissed the guards off because they were being right twats. Their use of unnecessary profanity was something that we were now used to but it reached its peak for the trip so far on this occasion. This outburst would, however, appear to be tame by the time the trip was over.

It was thirteen hours later when the papers were finally stamped and we were given permission to leave. We had not gotten out of the small confined space in all that time so we were all feeling worse for wear, all except the two who had been sipping coffee from the drinks machine in the customs offices. They jumped into their cab and she proudly exclaimed in a blatantly staged act how brilliant he was for successfully negotiating our release! Sharon and James looked at each other in stunned silence and I just held my breath. It was more of the same as we made our way through Hungary; but I did have lots of happy memories as I gazed out of the sticker-laden window.

Fifteen years ago when I was nine years old my uncle took me on a trip to Budapest to meet my aunt who was working at a special school in the capital. It was a great adventure for a nine-year-old.

On the way over it took only three days to get to Budapest and we stayed in really nice youth hostels with luxuries like beds. One scene I recalled is the large statue of a bronze eagle on the top of a hill as you look to the left on approaching the city. If you look to the right there is a nice looking house with lorries parked outside and women sitting in the upstairs windows. This sight was too much for a nine-year-old to comprehend, but quite a different matter fifteen years later and I almost suggested we pull in for lunch, and pudding! The only other thing that I remembered about Hungary is the great transportation infrastructure in the country. In Budapest, you could buy an all-day ticket for twenty pence and travel on the underground, the trams, the railway, electric buses and a cable car. I also recollect memories of a bridge that spans the Danube.

My uncle told me all about the chain bridge which is a brilliantly designed and ornately decorated construction which has been reliable for hundreds of years. When it was first built the man who designed it said that he believed it was flawless in design and if anyone could find fault with the elevated structure in any way he would throw himself from the bridge to his death. The first ten tears of the spans life went by with no critical comment and then one day a tourist noticed that the four marble lions that proudly guarded the bridge had no tongues. The next day the artisan, true to his word, threw himself from the bridge and was found dead. After my uncle told me this story I vowed to myself to never declare perfection, but to get as close to self-actualisation as possible.

It was great reliving all of the wonderful memories but it also brought back memories of a strict diet that I was on at the time.

I was starting to feel quite peckish and in the horizon I could see an amazing sight. There was a golden glow that grew brighter and brighter as we got closer and closer. It was like a mirage and I started to salivate at the thought of the impending golden arches. My strong power of visualisation clouded my mind with the image of a big, fat, juicy, tasty beef burger in a lightly toasted sesame seed bun with lettuce, tomatoes, gherkins, and mayonnaise oozing out of the side. That combined with lovely hot, crunchy, delectable French fries and a deliciously thick strawberry milkshake. Just the thought of it could be compared to paradise and made my glands go into overdrive. Saliva could be clearly seen flowing out of my mouth, and that was from the rear view mirror of the car in front!

I got on the CB with at least a mile to go and told the lead wagon that I needed to pull over at the next stop due to the fact that my physiological condition needed to be attended to. All teased me as I had mentioned for the last thousand miles that what I wanted most was a milkshake. The two were in the lead van and were about half a mile in front and they were rapidly approaching the turn off. They were not making any attempt to slow down and made no effort to lean, in fact they were as vertical as a skyscraper. At first I was concerned that they would topple over at the speed they were going when they turned off, but a worse fear was that they were not going to stop at all. That attestation was brought to reality with a thud when they zoomed past with a blatant nonchalant attitude. They did not want to stop and they knew that I did so they decided to play the control card.

My head slumped into the palm of my hands and despair was written across my face as the convoy speed past the services and the illuminated logo was just a flash of yellow light. I so longed for the thick solution to lap over my taste buds and the cravings were not helped by passing a McDonalds.

On Top of the World, Under a Lorry

I was hungry in Hungary and glad to be leaving it, but before we could there was the small obstacle of yet another border. I was not counting on this one to be easy. I should learn that you always get what you expect in life; and what you visualise, whether negative or positive, will come to fruition if you firmly believe in it. My subconscious had already made up its mind that this final frontier was going to be a long one.

Fourteen hours later, a bribe of a jar of coffee and a packet of cigarettes and we were through the first border but we still had the Romanian rim to contend with. We were told by a French lorry driver that the Hungarian border would always be difficult when humanitarian aid was involved as Hungary was not at peace with Romania and they didn't like Romanians receiving help. But the Romanian side should be no problem as long as we offered a gift to the guard.

The two minute ride in no-mans land was an exhilarating experience and in these precious seconds I could relate to the feelings of a freed prisoner who had surrendered his shackles. Just to be able to see the landscape moving out of the window was wonderful, as the same dull image had been stuck to the pane for hours. I had high expectations of breezing through the border as we were assisting their country and we had two packets of Rothmans ready.

There were three lorries in front of our vehicle so before checking in we all went to the currency kiosk. Sharon, James and I pooled our money together to avoid paying three separate commission rates. We each put thirty pounds into the pot and left it with James, our new financial advisor. We thought that thirty pounds would last for a few days and we might get a better rate in the town where shops would be competing for business. James came back from the kiosk a few minutes later with a huge smile on his face and a bigger bundle of cash in his hands. He had exactly three million, three hundred Lay which meant that we were each now millionaires. The exchange rate was 32,000 Lay to the pound. My wallet was bulging with notes and it was a great feeling having the most tangible cash ever in my possession.

When we approached the guard, our slippery leader slithered out from behind the wheel and walked up to the kiosk with a John Wayne swagger. He dumped the papers on the desk in front of the guard and slapped the cigarettes on top. He then pushed the fags towards the watchman and pointed at the papers. The guard took the gift and went away with the papers only to return ten minutes later. He gave him the papers back and pointed to a building in the corner of the car park. He sat back in his swivel chair and put his crossed feet up on his desk. He was lighting his first cigarette as we pulled away.

The two in the front sniggered at each other and said how great they were for getting us through so quick. There was a long tailback of lorries waiting for the exit and it took us over three hours to get to the front. We gave our papers to the man operating the barrier and he mumbled something and hit the papers with his fist several times to non-verbally communicate that the papers had not been stamped. The barrier stayed firmly shut and we were made to go back to where we began to do the system all over again, but this time making sure that the papers were stamped. The dusk was starting to settle and I realised it was going to be another day before the rubber tyres of our convoy touched Romanian soil.

I got my sleeping bag out of my sports bag and placed it in my bedroom which was positioned under the greasy axle of the lorry, but being positive I told myself that I wasn't just under a lorry, I was also on top of the world.

Romania Revisited

Fifteen hours after we left no-mans land we were going under the exit barrier to Romania. It was a great feeling and I felt like getting out of the van and kissing the floor. It was four in the morning and I thought we were on the final hurdle of our trip.

To the great surprise of the group we pulled in at a motel, which was less than half a mile from the border. There was a bright neon sign flashing outside and a large car park to the rear. There was only one straight road for the next hundred miles so it would have been impossible to deviate off the route. The vehicles had been impounded at the border but the passengers were free to cross over the edge at any time so everyone but the three drivers could have gone to the motel, especially the children, for a meal and a decent night's sleep. It was suggested two or three times but our wonderful leader said that we would not be able to find it and it was best if we all stayed together.

Before checking in for the rest of the day and the night I was accosted by a young child selling wooden pots and chessboards. Prices started at 200,000 Lay for a pot and 250,000 for a hand-made chessboard. Without a blink our leader had bought the two items and handed over 400,000 Lay. I managed to barter my way down to 90,000 before telling him that I did not want to buy anything, as I did not want to carry it around for the next three weeks, but I would make some purchases on our return.

James, Sharon and I decided that we would share a room and we were shocked to find that a room for the night with breakfast would cost us 200,000 Lay each! It took a few minutes to realise that this was only seven pounds but it was also a fifth of our currency. It was also a shock because at the initial brief we were told that a room would cost a lot less, but then nothing they had told us had yet to come to fruition.

At first, the lady at reception did not want to serve us as we were in a large group and insisted that the whole group of thirteen pay the 200,000 Lay each and use only two rooms, but when I picked my money up and started to walk away, she gave in.

Within minutes we were in our plain white room that was sparsely decorated but fairly clean, and of course there was the ethereal rectangular object that I had longed for and within seconds I had my head on the pillow into one of my dream worlds complete with beautiful bronzed women on white sandy beaches.

Six hours had passed when the sound of the shower pounding down woke me from my heavenly slumber. Through the frosted glass I could see the outline of Sharon's body. I quickly averted my gaze and put my head back under the sheets. From the small bathroom that was located at the base of my bed I could hear groaning sounds followed by an abrupt scream. I looked around the room and James was nowhere to be seen. I was just about to get my tape recorder out to use as evidence when James walked into the room quite happily with his camera hung around his neck and his sandals flopping about on his feet. Seconds later Sharon emerged from the shower with a sigh saying that that was the most invigoratingly hot shower she had ever had, until the thermostat broke and the water went ice cold.

I was the last to use the bathroom and when I flushed the toilet nothing happened. My first thoughts were that this was a continental type amenity and I had to do something strange to get it to operate, but when the tap would not function I realised that the water had gone off. This was the first of many times whilst in Romania that I would have problems with water. Just having the facilities to accommodate running water was a luxury but it was not advised to consume it. Bottled water was readily available in the shops and service stations in the fridges bearing the distinctive red flowing Coca-Cola logo. It was worth the small cost of the containers as I once had a shower some years ago with my mouth open whilst in Kenya and ended up with stomach cramps for a week.

What's That Smell?

I didn't bother with a wash so went down to dinner with an off-putting aroma surrounding me. It brought back memories of a New Year's Eve when for the first time in my life I had inadvertently consumed an illegal substance that was present in a rather tasty chocolate cake. All I can remember is the floor going wobbly beneath me, then my head started spinning and I blanked out. When I came round I was violently sick, but I wasn't in the small London flat with the scrumptious buffet, I was on a train headed towards Trafalgar Square. The train was packed with thousands of partygoers, all in high spirits. It was standing room only with people tightly huddled together like the proverbial sardines in a tin can, and the cabin did smell quite fishy come to think about it. The constricted coach was dispersed like fox running from the hounds when I vomited over everyone within arms reach. The groans from all the passengers and looks of disgust were coming at me from all angles, but no one had the intestinal fortitude to get too close. From then on and for the rest of the evening in jam packed London a path would clear before me like Moses separating the waves.

I hadn't had a proper wash in nearly a week and when the opportunity was there, the water was not. We had a nice meal and a few drinks which cost less than a pound before retiring for the night on what we hoped was the last night of travelling. We were up at seven in the morning expecting a nice breakfast and were disappointed to find that it was bread with jam and a cup of tea. I had imagined a plate of sizzling bacon and eggs, but instead we were greeted by bread that was over a week old. After breakfast we went back to our room and got our things together. The time was rapidly approaching eight o'clock and we were all ready for the final lap of the journey. We were hopeful that by the time the sun had set, we would be at our destination, Brazov, Romania.

I may have been ready, and most of the team were chomping at the bit like caged greyhounds waiting for the rabbit to be let loose, but our leaders were not. They didn't get out of bed until ten thirty and made no attempt to hurry. He came down the stairs in full view of everyone wearing nothing but a dirty pair of shorts and a string vest. His beer belly was flopping out and a fag was tentatively dangling from his bottom lip. He grunted at us as we waited patiently to depart, then wiped the mucus from his eyes, coughed and went to indulge in the stale bread and jam. She then came down in a tight pair of shorts, which were bursting at the seams; the small metal button holding the shorts up was in obvious distress and if it could verbally communicate would just scream in pain. She made some disturbing noises with her posterior, feeling proud of her musical talents she went of to breakfast laughing.

We did not leave until they had had one more coffee, which was just past one o'clock. My fingers were sore from twiddling and my head was aching from the feeling of stagnation. The mood of the group was not what I would call enthusiastic, although it should have been. We had finally reached Romania, we were all in good health despite sleeping rough and our destination was within our grasp. Everyone seemed like they had been conditioned to reform into a state of negativity just so they would not have their hopes dashed next time something would inevitably go wrong. I almost considered starting a book.

What Are the Chances of That Happening?

I went off into one of my trances as I considered the odds that I could offer. 100 to1 war would break out, 66 to1 we would get to our destination safely by nightfall, 6 to1 we would not get there at all, 3 to 1 our leader would have a heart attack and die and odds on favourite, offering even money, that the van would break down yet again. This consideration did not last too long as I knew that everyone would have placed money on the van failing. The probability of which was more than highly likely, also, because our leader was so devious he would have probably bet money on him having a heart attack and then fake his own death!

Time for Coffee

After just three hours it was time for our now routine coffee break, which would last for over two hours. The quality of the roadside stops was starting to deteriorate. In Europe we were treated to large service stations with great facilities, shower rooms and a choice of restaurants. Now we had a roadside shed with some woman in her late seventies offering cans of pop and a homemade cheese sandwich. After looking at her culinary delights, I had to question whether it was cheese at all and I wondered where she obtained it. It looked more like the fresh cream coloured scrapings from the bottom of her smelly feet. If it was cheese, then it was certainly more mature than the woman herself. I had eaten a plate of chips at nearly every stop and this was the first time that I declined food so it was good in a way that the quality was starting to deteriorate as I needed to lose some weight!

The next six hours went quite smoothly by recent standards. James and I went in the God mobile and Dave was driving. His wife and kids were travelling in the little cell behind the cab, which had now become a familiar surrounding for them and they accepted it as their playroom. We managed 300 miles with only one short stop and things were starting to look up. James suggested that we swap drivers and keep going, to our great surprise everyone agreed. Over 500 miles in one day was totally unheard of and this new wave of freshness brought with it a tide of vivacity. We were now only 200 miles away from our final destination on day eight of our traumatic travels and it was looking like we would make the children's home that was to be our base by nightfall.

The Hero's Return!

We were driving along a lovely Romanian cobbled road with little houses on either side with women sitting in groups making lace blankets. It was a picturesque scene that would have made a lovely oil painting. There was a gentle breeze gushing through the vehicle as our leaders had the windows to the van wide open. It was not fresh air that they were after, but glory. They would beep their horn at all the people as we slowly drove by and they leaned out of the window waving as if they were a president on a ceremonial tour. They said that all of the people had come out of their houses because they knew we would be driving along and they came out to greet us as they helped them the year before.

I could see that they honestly believed that they were mighty warriors or saviours making a triumphant return, and should have been placed on an open top bus, but I realised that they believed a lot of things about themselves that could not be further from the truth. Looking out of the van, between the mazes of car stickers, I could see puzzled looks on the faces of the Romanians and realised that they did not have a clue who, or what we were. They were not waving back, just fanning the exhaust emissions from the van away from their faces.

A mile further down the road there were two people standing by a car and they frantically waved us down. The brakes on the van screeched as we abruptly came to a halt. Moans filled the air as we all wanted to get on but he insisted that they needed our help. The pair of well dressed German men mumbled softly in broken English that they desperately needed to change their Marks for Romanian currency and they would give us over the odds just to get some Lay. Alarm bells started ringing in the ears of everyone, everyone except one man. He said that if you couldn't help a German tourist in need, then who could you help!

The German got a bundle of Marks out and said thank you three times before saying just 500,000 Lay. The dope put his hand into his bum bag, pulled out a wad of Romanian notes and promptly handed it over. The faces of everyone in the van fell into open cupped hands with shakes of disbelief. When he returned, feeling very proud of himself for helping yet another person, James said he should see how much he had made, as he had his currency converter on him. He said that there was no need as he had already worked out that he had done well, and he had just made money out of a load of bloody Germans. She suggested that James just quickly check it, so he threw the money over his shoulder in a blasé manner. James double checked it, handed it back and said nothing.

Silence remained for the next few minutes until she could not keep it up any longer, and looked over her shoulder from the front seat and simply asked, "Well?"

"Well what?" came the response and she demanded to know how much he had made.

The brakes screeched and brought the van to another abrupt halt, throwing his false teeth out of his mouth and onto the windscreen as James said that it was not even worth five pounds. A quick u-turn and an anger induced acceleration resulted in a further delay. It felt like we were sliding down a snake when we should have been conquering a ladder.

The Germans were nowhere to be seen and he suggested that we all chip in to make up for his loss. This was countered with gasps of amazement followed by tones of disenchantment. We kept going in the wrong direction for a further ten minutes when it was suggested that we turn around and just accept the fact that his stupidity had cost him dear.

Nine days of exhaustion were starting to take their toll and grey hairs were starting to sprout from the left side of my head. I had to tell myself that tough times don't last, but tough people do as I plucked each of the discoloured hairs from my head. I had to borrow Sharon's small vanity mirror that she kept in her handbag to do this task and it shook so violently as the van trundled along that my reflection was just a hazy blur. I think I must have pulled at least thirty good hairs for each grey coloured one, and there were six of those.

Dusk was starting to fall and our destination was getting closer as the day was getting darker. The convoy was now halfway up a large hill with winding roads and beautiful panoramic views of Romania. It was great to see the many rural villages, the cornfields and the stone walls, but what was even better was seeing our goal in sight, a goal that we had been aiming at for so many days. On the other side of the hill we were told that we'd be able to see Brazov, which would be our new home for a week.

Excitement was starting to grow, and the collective feeling of exhilaration was so tangible that if I had a knife I could have cut it up and eaten it. Looking out of the dirty, dust laden, sticker covered window was the beautifully romantic orange coloured sun that was slowly descending behind the imposing hill in front of us, making silhouettes of the trees on the side of the snake like road.

The mood could not be spoilt, the setting was perfect, we were within an hour of reaching our goal and spirits were high. Then there was a clanking sound from under the van and smoke coming from the bonnet. Did I say the mood could not be spoilt? Like a needle scratching in the middle of a love tune vinyl, the ambience was shattered.

I almost expected a bright yellow blow up slide to inflate when we all made an emergency escape out of the side door, dashing to the safety of a nearby cherry bush. Nobody felt secure in the van when it was running well, but when it was making obscene noises and producing an array of visual stimulation not seen since the special effects team left the James Bond set, then there was definite uneasiness. Revolt was on everyone's mind when he said that we might as well bed down for the night and sort the van out in the morning. I did not want to spend another night out in the elements so I suggested that we utilise the vehicles that were working, and leave the van there. He said that he was not going to leave his van, so I then suggested that he stay with the van and everyone else just carry on. It looked like someone had screwed the lid off a pressurised container as the anxiety on the faces of Sharon and James was lifted. Everyone agreed that it was a great idea, all except for the two of them who said we should stay together.

We were all back into the workable convoy before they had a chance to argue and the horn of the lead wagon was soon heard belting out its distinctive call. Geoff took control and was soon blazing the trail for the others to follow. In the time of despair he had stepped forward and decided to become a leader. James was sitting next to him in the lorry and I was lying on his camper style bed behind the two seats.

We started chatting about the trip, our thoughts and how our faith in aid trips had been dashed. Geoff then started to cry, and became ever so emotional as he said that he could barely cover the amount needed to come on the trip, and he had taken out a small loan to cover the costs just because he wanted to do something worthwhile. He then sniffled a few times, wiped the tears away with a hanky and told us that he recently learnt that he could not have children, and that's why his fiancé had left him. All he wanted to do was help them. He also said that he could give a lovely home, lots of love and joy to some orphans if he could only get them back to England.

James and I were now hit by another swerve ball. Not only were the people who had organised the trip totally incompetent, but one of the volunteers was contemplating child smuggling!

We've Made It!

I don't know how we did it, but we arrived at the tall closed gates to the children's home without even having to ask for directions. Geoff's lorry was like a laser-guided missile, hitting its target with pinpoint accuracy. I wished that I had the attitude of a projectile being able to aim for a goal without procrastinating, being distracted or coming up with lame excuses.

I've often kicked myself years after making a naff rationale as to why I couldn't do something only to realise that I could and if I had just gone on and done it, my life would have been so much richer.

The gates were locked with a rusty brass bolt and catch. I wasn't sure if this was to stop the children getting out or to prevent intruders from breaking in. I peered through the tall tarnished bars. There was a long straight driveway with conifers either side that led to a large menacing stone built edifice that was used to house the unwanted children. The drive had acres of grassland around it, which was long, unkempt and obviously unused.

I started to go into one of my visionary modes and thought about all the good we could do in the week that we were there. Firstly, we could put an adventure playground in one corner and build a small farm with hens and sheep. We could also create a wildlife pond and a football pitch. I had a warm glow developing inside and thought that all the hassle would be worth it because of the difference we would make to the lives of the children.

Within a few minutes of us inspecting the lock, trying to work out how you get a fifty foot lorry through the bars, a gorgeous, but very shy woman in her early twenties came out of a building just to the side of the driveway. She was dressed a bit like a nurse with a figure hugging white dress and paper hat. I immediately noticed that she had purple hands, which really stood out against the starched dress. Her English was broken, but I thought that was cute. She told us that she would be looking after us for the week and she would make sure the children were kept out of our way. She also thanked us for all the work that we were going to do and if we wanted anything then to just ask.

She suggestively rolled her hair around her fingers as she said this and I went into one of my now legendary trances. I won't say what was going through my mind but when I came back to the real world my whole body was covered in purple patches.

Nice Room!

We were escorted inside the menacing building at the end of the driveway. There was a huge hall with black and white chequered floor tiles and a large oak fireplace. The walls were lined with wooden panels and there was an expansive stairway, but total silence. It reminded me of a stately room in an old castle. I asked where the children were and was told that they were upstairs and fast asleep despite the fact that it was now the middle of the afternoon.

Through the banisters at the top of the stairs I could see a little girl peering through the wooden poles. They looked more like constrictive bars on a prison cell than protective trusses to keep her safe. She was dressed in a dirty white un-matching pyjama set, and her face was discoloured with a purple dye. I wanted to reach out to the cute little girl but she was pulled away by one of the matrons and she disappeared round a corner.

In the distance, down the long driveway I could see a grey cloud of smoke that encapsulated a welded, bolted and strung together van. As it veered round a corner I could see her leaning out of the window to aid the suspension and I realised that they'd caught us up. Peace was now over. Anarchy was about to resume. Everyone started to cough as clouds of exhaust smoke, now mixed with dirt, tar and bits of tree, enveloped us as they came to a screeching halt.

They jumped out and asked where their rooms were as they wanted to lie down. I jumped in and asked when we were going to see the children because I wanted to start making a difference. Our leader said the children would only get in the way, and they'd just be a nuisance! Here I was thousands of miles from home to help children in need, and I was told that it would be best to stay away from them.

My blood was about to boil when five children bolted down the stairs and headed straight for me. I would have been overcome with joy and elation, but I didn't have time as two of the children grabbed my left leg, two seized the bottom half of my right leg and one just gripped onto my arm and began swinging. They were holding me like they had never been cuddled before and were in desperate need of affection. I found this heart rendering and emotive, that is until another ten children saw what was going on and made a dash for

52

me. I had them draping from nearly every part of my body. If there was space to clip a clothes peg then there was room for another child. My internal love and kindness felt like it was being gang mugged! It took Geoff, James and three heavy duty matrons to get the children off and I felt a morsel of shame from the relief I was experiencing as they each released their leech like grip. All the children wanted was some tenderness, and I was brushing them off like bobbles on a well-worn woolly jumper.

Perfect Planning Prevents...

My bedroom was facing East so the dawn cracking over the mountainous Romanian horizon like a freshly laid free range egg woke me up early. I jumped out of bed with a mixture of excitement and eagerness at the prospect of starting to build a playground or farm for the children. I hastily got dressed and ran out onto the large concrete veranda at the front of the building with a sketchbook and pen and started to plan where everything would go.

Hours passed as I inked in the details with the precision that is normally carried out by a neurosurgeon planning a major operation. The sun was shining high in the sky by the time my plan was in place and the rest of the group strolled out to catch some rays. I proudly showed off my masterpiece and was about to delegate jobs when he came pounding out in his string vest, cigarette dangling from his mouth and supping a stained plastic cup full of coffee. He told us that we wouldn't be hanging around at the orphanage today but donating the clothing supplies to the needy. I was a little disappointed but reasoned that we could build the farm tomorrow. Making the needy more comfortable was a good thing to do.

Reverend Birch Bojangles

After an hour's journey through a maze of small cobbled streets full of houses that seemed to require lots of maintenance, we arrived at a grand looking avenue with houses that appeared to be on the plush side of luxurious. I thought we were being taken on a historical tour of Romania but was shocked to learn that we had reached our destination. Before the dust settled on the banged up brake pads, a portly, well-dressed man came out and greeted our leader with a hearty hand shake. A smart looking woman of equal proportions closely followed but ignored everyone and made a beeline for the back of the van. She could hardly contain herself as she swung opened the heavy metal doors and started sifting through the bags of clothing.

We were told that this was the Reverend Birch Bojangles and his adoring wife Debrisals. They were apparently leading missionaries in the area and had devoted their entire lives to helping others, but from their appearance it seemed that they were committed to just one thing, eating!

We were told to unload the clothing into their garage and as we worked up a sweat they went in for lunch, only to come out an hour later wearing different clothes. Birch grinned in my direction and a glimmer of light reflected on what I'm sure was a gold tooth. This made me look at his hands and they were covered in gold rings. Things didn't feel at all right and when he gave our leader a thin sealed envelope and a brown packaged box, the cogs started to turn in my head.

T.B. or Not T.B.

The original plan was to work for three days and have a day off, maybe even take in some of the sights as a reward for all our hard work. But, as I'd learned from past experience, what was set in stone could easily be chiselled out, and our leaders were expert stone masons. The new plan was to work for a day and then take three days off. I couldn't start work on the playground because all of the gardening kit and toys were strategically placed in the lorry behind a ton of bathroom items for the tuberculosis hospital. The order was given that we'd complete my plans after we'd refurbished the toilets for the needy patients. Again I could see the benefit in this so jumped in the lorry when the order was given.

We eventually got to the T.B. hospital several days later, and were greeted by dozens of ill looking people walking around with drips that appeared to be Victorian in character. The medical feeders found in hospitals in England are normally polished, shiny chrome with a paperclip on top, but these were brown, rusty and ornate in design. I looked around to find the rest of the team. Sharon and James were already shaking hands with the ailing inmates, but our leaders were peering over the bonnet of their van wearing heavy duty gas masks! The faces of the patients were frail and yellow and they all moved slowly, in groups of four and five and all wore dressing gowns. The similarities didn't end there as all the men had a moustache and all were smoking woodbines.

The senior doctor came out wearing a dazzling white coat and greeted us with the enthusiasm that I normally save for a free Christmas meal. It was obvious that he was glad to see us as he led us down a corridor to a large locked door, as he was skipping most of the way. There was lots of 1960s designer furniture in the halls and I could hear the two talking about the market for it back at home.

The doctor slowly unlocked the door, which built up the tension, and then opened it even more deliberately to a particularly loud creak. If I'd had something to bang I'd have given him a drum roll as we all wanted to know what was behind it. However, when it was revealed, none of us wanted to know. The pungent aroma of stale urine wafted through the air. There were cobwebs everywhere and the plaster was falling from the walls. This was the toilet that they wanted us to refurbish, but I knew that we'd only be here for two days, and from looking around, it would take at least a month to make it presentable.

One thing that I've learnt from others wiser than me is that when you set your goals, make them realistic and achievable, and never start something that you know you won't conclude. If we'd had a month to spare then I'd eagerly start to scrape down the walls, but with just a short time before we'd be off, I could hardly see the point. The decision was made, however, by our ubiquitous leader, and within five minutes they were banging, cutting and scraping away.

Three hours had passed and the room was looking far worse than before we began. The toilets that at least worked had been removed, plaster had been slapped on the walls over the damp patches and the some of the broken tiles had been chipped from the walls, despite the fact that we had nothing to put in their place. Dust was flying everywhere and vision was down to about five inches, which was the only positive thing!

By the next day things had not improved, in fact it turned out to be worse. There was a huge pile of rubble in the corner of the room where the showers once stood and debris was hanging from the wall. I thought to myself that an alternative artist at the Tate Modern would probably be proud of this creation, and display it in a large white room with a plaque. But this was no work of art. It was supposed to be a clean convenience and it resembled a bomb shelter that had been the target of a direct hit.

Footsteps could be heard coming closer down the corridor to the joyful sounds of a happy hum. The smartly suited head doctor that had greeted us so positively on our arrival obviously had visions of grand designs floating around in his brain, and the prediction of a changing room style makeover, complete with wall hangings and the traditional finishing off touch, a floral design. As we were far from finishing, there was a distinct lack of flower pots let alone blooms of any description, but there was plenty of mud! When the doctor peered his head around the corner of the door the tuneful hum stopped with a sudden silence. His face, which was quite rosy in complexion, had instantly drained of any colour and was now matching the starchiness of his coat. His vision of a state-of-the-art washroom with electric hand dryers had become nothing short of a nightmare. He didn't say anything, but the cupped hands covering his face made up for the lack of words. He looked around, thumped the wall and slowly walked away muttering miserably.

I could relate to the way he was feeling, and totally understood his state of mind, but I could never let my frustrations boil to the surface in the way that he did. I would much rather inhale a few deep breaths, think about the situation logically and then calmly work out a solution. I did this and found myself hitting the wall for the first time, splattering semi dried plaster all over the floor! I've since learnt to never be disappointed when others let you down. Just make sure you do your best not to fail others and under no circumstances let yourself down. If you say you're going to do it, like slimming or giving up cigarettes, then you just do it.

Within a few minutes of the doctor departing dejectedly, we were closely behind and jumping in our van, leaving behind a building site, a large cloud of dust and a few shattered dreams.

Still No Playground, but a New Leader!

We were running short of time and the mission had less life in it than a rotting corpse, so Geoff decided to drive straight to Bucharest as it was only a few hours away. The rest of the team had no choice but to agree as he had the keys and the control to the vehicle, which contained all the remaining aid.

I had the urge to go back to the children's home in Brazov to develop my playground, but that would mean driving back overnight and it didn't make logistical sense. Before I had chance to mull over the alternatives a loud horn bellowed across the nearby valley. It roared from the top of the articulated vehicle as a symbolic sound to signify leadership. This was intermingled with the thunderous reverberation of the air brakes easing off and the wagons started to roll.

Within seconds we were heading north to the capital city. We were headed straight towards another children's home that was run by a British charity, but this time with our new caretaker team leader we had focus, vision and direction. This didn't sit too well with the two of them as they were well overdue a coffee and fag break. Within a few hours of departing the order came over the radio to pull over at the next stop, but as the service station could be seen getting closer on the horizon, so could the pressure on Geoff's acceleration peddle. He once again honked a loud ten second blast on his horn as he swiftly thundered past the exit with a combination of courage and defiance.

I found a small scrap of paper that was left over from the children's creative spur a few hours ago, and as I was personally proud of Geoff's newfound attitude began to draw an alternative portrait of him as a tribute. I firstly picked up an orange pen and drew the body of a lion to represent the audacity and boldness he was displaying. Instead of drawing a cat like head with long flowing main, I instead put a spotty, greasy haired teenager to characterize his rebelliousness and as a finishing touch, a Yorkshire style flat cap.

City Sights

We arrived in Bucharest well ahead of the time we all expected to. This meant that we possessed a few valuable hours until we could proceed to the children's home so we decided to have a look around. James and Sharon set off to find one of the many ornately decorated churches. The family wanted to find a burger bar as they were getting ravenous especially the youngest that was starting to stamp his feet. Geoff wanted to treat himself to a new tweed jacket and the two were desperate to get some cheap fags.

I went on my own to check out the transport infrastructure, which I expected to be quite basic but was amazed to find that it outclassed anything that a British city had to offer. First I hopped onto one of the many orange coloured caterpillar buses, which was twice the length of a normal one but hinged in the centre. Then I took a trip on the underground before popping onto a tram, going for a ride up the mountain on a train and coming down on a cable car. All this for the price of a one day ticket, which was about twenty pence. The whole system ran smoothly and totally outshined anything that I'd experienced before.

We all met back up at three in the afternoon and swapped the experiences that we had acquired. I told of my travel exploits, James was buzzing about his spiritual encounter and the two had bags of shopping, brimming with cut price cigarettes and whiskey bottles.

Many Happy Nuns!

I was given the job of map reading from the city to the home and only made a few schoolboy errors which were quickly conquered. Nothing a few extra left turns couldn't correct.

I thought about all the mistakes that I had made previously on my journey through life, and how they didn't really matter because I knew where I was going. But what happens when you take a wrong turning and you don't have a dream or goal? You could be going the wrong way for a lifetime without even realising it.

We drove down a shabby looking side street made up of caravan type homes and pulled up outside a modern looking brick building with large glass windows. It was a stark contrast to the other home that we had stayed at earlier and was like comparing a top of the range Rolls Royce to a home made go-cart.

We walked into a large airy entrance hall that was adorned with pictures the children had made. They were brightly coloured and included smiling faces and balloons, which created very good, positive vibes. We were greeted by an extremely pleasant English lady who welcomed us into the centre and gave us a tour around. It was inharmoniously quiet and from my experience at the other home asked if the children were all asleep. She replied that it was far too early for bed and they were all having a quick splash at the local swimming pool. There was a lovely dining room, a relaxation lounge with television and a fully fitted kitchen. The rooms upstairs were spacious and nicely decorated and it had the ambience of a family home. I settled down in the lounge and drifted off into a soothing slumber.

I was looking forward to going into one of my wild and wacky creative dreams but was suddenly woken by a group of children running through the door straight past me and into the kitchen. Before I had chance to look around a soft, tender hand was embracing my shoulder and a mixture of white cloth and brown hair lightly fell over my face like a tranquil stream rippling over a weir.

A gorgeous young looking nun sat on the arm of my chair and greeted me with a dazzling white smile that lit up the room far brighter than a halo ever could. She said in a very sexy, broken English inflection that her name was

Gabby. She'd be looking after us for the next few days and if there was anything she could do to make my stay more comfortable, then to simply ask. I was just about to invite her out for dinner when I realised that not only was she a woman of the cloth, but from the aroma drifting round the room and lingering tantalisingly around the base of my nose, lunch was about to be served anyway.

I got to know Gabby really well over the next few days, and made up for the team's lack of missionary work with some positions of a homonymous nature. We also talked for hours about her life and growing up in Romania. She made it clear that it was not easy for young women like her to get by in Romania with low pay and inadequate housing, but the quality of life when in the Church was quite nice. Young girls would sign up just because they could guarantee warmth, food and clothing. She said that she missed what others would call a normal way of life, and in the three days I spent at the home she more than made up for it.

On our last day I had to tear myself away. I had grown fond of the children who were polite and friendly and Sister Gabriella, who could be described as a wild tiger in sheep's clothing. Before I could finally pack my bags she scribbled a German address on an old sweet wrapper and asked me to meet her there in three week's time. She said it was her brother's home. She was allowed to visit him once a year and she would run away to England with me when she got there!

Before too long we were all back into our selection of vehicles and Geoff's distinctive horn bellowed vociferously. It was my turn to drive the God mobile, but just before Geoff had the chance to rev up his engines I jumped out from behind my wheel and told him that I had lost my tiepin, which was a family heirloom and asked if I could see if was in his truck. He didn't mind but pondered as to why I was wearing a tiepin when I didn't even have a tie. He bought my good luck story and I searched around his cab like an investigator at a crime scene. I hadn't really lost anything but wanted to make sure he had not tried to smuggle any of the children!

Crash

Our way back to the original base in Brazov was fraught with more danger and strife than most snipers experience in a lifetime of overseas service! We were used to things not going our way, but nothing could mentally prepare us for what lay ahead.

First of all the wheel to our large lorry hit a pothole on the ropey Romanian road and violently swerved on impact. It nearly jack-knifed but Geoff's expertise and genuine love of his vehicle avoided what could have been a nasty incident. He calmly pulled the truck over to the side and onto a dirt track that had the tyre indentations of the countless past vehicles that had followed the same routine. The scores of swerve marks on the road had made a groove on the tarmac which acted as a mini reservoir, or a bath for thrill seeking birds whenever it rained. It was as if there was an emergency safety guide tucked in front of the driver's seat, like the ones found on aircraft that told them which escape route they should follow.

Geoff was visibly traumatized by what had happened. His hands were shaking, his teeth chattered and he was inhaling slightly deeper than normal. The combined noises he was turning out sounded like an electronic beat box and would have made any half-talented rap artist proud. Sharon went over to Geoff, hovered her fingers over his head and started humming in what was calculated to be a calming act of caring. It seemed to be working as the regularity of his rhythm was decreasing in tempo.

We all stood in a group, lapping up the soothing vibes that Sharon was emitting when a car whizzed by on the wrong side of the road and crashed into an oncoming vehicle. The restful atmosphere was shattered into a thousand pieces like a mirror being dropped from a great height when the impact made a deafening blast. Debris flew past us like tomatoes being thrown at a bad performer and luckily missed us all. I could see a shard of orange plastic from one of the indicator lights bed itself into a nearby tree. As the sap was flowing from the open lesion and the bark round the edges of the wound started to fray, I thought to myself that it could easily have been my skin that was pierced if it were not for the great mighty oak standing in the way like a knight in shining armour. I started to once again get goose bumps on my arm, which reminded me of the sensation that I experienced on the first day of the trip as the rain pounded down.

I almost began to wish that I could turn the clock back to that day, and thought about all the things that I would have done differently, but remembered the advice that I had given to so many other people. Don't wish for something you can't have, only dream for things that you can have, then set about getting them.

One thing that we all needed to do with urgency was to help out the injured people. The car that was struck was now face down in a ditch to the side of the road. There was smoke rising from under the crumpled bonnet; dents and depressions, far greater than that of the injured people's mindset were running in uniformed patters down both sides of the vehicle and all the windows were smashed.

Our two leaders ran in the other direction for fear of the car exploding, but Sharon and I rushed over after a second of contemplation to get the injured out. Sharon tried to undo the driver side door but it would not open. I also tried with all my might, but, like trying to release Merlin's sword out of a stone. It would not budge. I ran back to the God mobile, which seemed to have a bright yellow glow around it to try and find some tools. Taz was in the back with the mum and four young children. They were all crying from what they had seen, all except for the youngest son who was whining for some sweets. I had half a packet of mints in my pocket so I threw them at him in a gesture of good will. I was also used to just giving in to him to keep the noise levels down and the ranting to a minimum. As soon as the young one clasped the herbal confectionary, he started to laugh and threw a large metal object back at me in an act of defiance. It was the most useful thing that he had never intended to do as the item was a heavy duty wrench.

I ran back to the car, which was slowly sinking into the muddy ditch and Sharon was administering first aid through the fissure where a window once transparently sat. The man behind the wheel looked in a right mess. He was blood splattered, bruised and unconscious. This to me was a blessing in disguise as at least he didn't have to experience the shock, distress, and suffering from the situation he was in.

I thought about the many miracles in masks that had come my way over the years, like the time in primary school when the teacher thought I lacked the intelligence to move up a class. I was distraught at first, but when I found out that I would be sitting next to the prettiest girl in the school I started to learn the lesson that every cloud has a silver lining. There was also the time that a business associate I trusted inherently did me wrong to get a bigger slice of the cake, so I left the trade and moved onto to bigger and better things. Within months the industry was experiencing a state of depression and she went on to lose a lot of money. There are many blessings in disguises happening to each of us every day, but most of the time we don't really look hard enough to find them. If you miss the bus, the piece of good fortune may be that you can meet new people who are waiting for the next bus, or if you get made redundant at work, the boon could be that your ideal job is waiting round the corner.

I stuck the sharp end of the wrench into a small opening at the side of the door and put all my weight against it. Sharon also started to heave against me, groaning loudly as we collectively tried to ease the door open. The harmless smoke from under the bonnet was increasing in both density and danger, and the flicker of small flames could be seen coming out of the grill at the front of the car. It was now a necessity, not an option, to get the man out as quickly as possible.

When I caught sight of the conflagration coming from the vehicle, my body went into superhuman, almost hulk like mode. The shirt wasn't literally ripping off my back and my skin wasn't turning green, just an off shade of purple as I somehow managed to prise the door open. This taught me that if the desire is big enough, and the urgency is there then the job can and will get done.

We dragged the man to safety and an ambulance arrived followed closely by the blue flashing lights and loud screeching siren of the local police force. They pushed us to the side and got to work on the wreckage, making sure it was safe and the injured were tendered and taken away. Within an hour there was total calm. The damaged vehicles had been towed away and cars were passing at speed as if nothing had happened. We were all standing there in a state of semi-shock, but I pondered to myself how quickly the world moves on and how time really does heal all wounds.

The Terrible Two Turn

The journey continued, but much more carefully and cautiously than before. The two had no compassion for the people who had been hurt, and argued that if the victims had stuck to their fifty mile an hour rule then they would all be safe now. Our leader also suggested that we should keep the speed to below forty miles an hour and ordered Taz to lean out of the window to keep an eye out for pot holes and crazy drivers.

Sharon, James and I were sitting in the back of the van watching their comedic antics like thespians at a slapstick production. I felt slightly devilish so decided to change from a mere spectator to being part of the farce. I delved into the tool box at my side, which had varied on the journey from a hard pillow to a footstool for my weary feet. This was the first time ever I had used it for its intended purpose to see if there were any devices that would aid Taz in her mission to keep us safe. I looked past the varied array of screwdrivers and spanners, and was amused to see a shiny brass horn with a large red rubber honker. I mused to myself how this air filled instrument probably wouldn't keep us afloat if we splashed into a canal, but it would make the next few hours in the van far more amusing.

Before I had a chance to give the rubber sphere a sexual squeeze the brakes were forced and we were all thrown forward. Had Taz seen a pothole in the road? Had we just been saved by her new found lighthouse keeper type role? No, our leader had spotted a service station in the distance and was in need of a caffeine intake. Far from helping to avoid a further incident, Taz almost became one as her body, still leaning out of the window whilst driving on a major road, was contorted when the van swerved towards the distinctive aroma of freshly brewed beans.

The short, supposedly thirst quenching stop went on and on for what seemed like days, but was actually about four hours. At the beginning of the trip I had resented them for wasting my precious time, but one thing that I always try and do is to monitor my emotions to make sure that they're being directed for maximum effect, and that is to always keep me happy, healthy and wealthy.

Resentment, like hate, anger and jealousy is a negative emotion and a feeling like that can't possibly make you happy, so why have it in the first place. If I ever start to experience any disparaging feelings then I immediately think about constructive thoughts to replace them with. Why be sad when you can just as easily be happy? What's the point in looking back when it takes the same amount of time as planning for the future, and why have resentment when you can simply have love? Now I wasn't about to jump into bed with the two of them just to prostitute my negative thinking, but I did want to consider ways to thank them for their actions. No longer were they wasting days of my life stuck in petrol stations when I wanted to be helping needy children and genuinely making a difference. Now they were giving me time to learn about diverse parts of the world, time to read books and time to study the habits of lorry drivers!

Learn From a Lorry Driver

Truckers are a very interesting species quite unique in their outlook to life and with some very unusual habits. From my experience they all seem to have a fascination with decorative light bulbs, and like to hang them from every possible aperture and get particularly excited if they flash. The majority also like to wear padded check shirts, jeans held up by oversized brass buckled belts, and baseball caps with a space in the back for their hair to flow through. More importantly, despite any of their superficial shortcomings, they have an extraordinary attribute. They all support each other. They have developed their own community which appears to be devoid of any discrimination. No matter what corner of the globe you come from, what colour your skin is or what dialect you speak, if you wear a checked shirt and your lights twinkle then you're part of the family. They look out for each other on the road, radio to each other if there are problems ahead and support and socialise with each other. They don't even have to meet in person. They still share information which will make everybody's existence easier. Wouldn't life be wonderful if everyone adopted the philosophies of the humble articulated operator, not to mention more dazzling as well from all those flashing bulbs?

You're certainly never alone if you're a lorry driver, and I was about to lose my solitude as the group all strolled out of the café. The two and Taz had fags dangling from their mouths; the family were all covered in condiment stains and Sharon and James were relaxed and revitalised from a frolic in the fields. Everyone seemed to be in good spirits and I put it down to my attitude adjustment and positive paradigm shift. We all skipped our way to the assemblage of vehicles, singing to upbeat Abba tunes and all chatting amiably for the first time on the trip. I was feeling so good natured that in a moment of unharnessed consideration agreed to give the mother a break, and look after the children in the box at the back of the God mobile.

It was my first experience of cramping into what had become the four children's playroom, complete with en suit in the style of an empty energy drink bottle! I had to cram through the small side door, which I did with all the refinement of an elephant on ice. I honestly felt like a square peg trying to fit into a round hole, when in reality I was a rotund form trying to squeeze into a rectangular outline. I finally managed to get in and the door was bolted behind me to the combined clicking sound of a mortise being locked. I now had no way of getting out until I was released and felt more like a prisoner than I did when I was being transported in the former mobile cell. A small, cheap looking battery operated light illuminated the undersized area, but I think it would have been kinder to treat the children like veal. We played for a bit doing dot to dot and colouring, until the vibration from the lorry made it impossible to keep within the lines. Even my attempts to create a colourful masterpiece ended up looking the work of a five-month-old with a blunt crayon. The constant hum of the axle rotating underneath us and the frustration from not being able to complete a comprehensive picture sent the children off to sleep. Within minutes I was resting my head on a spare tyre and snoozing with the children compactly scattered around me.

I was awoken by the two eldest children and felt a screaming pain in my collar bone. If I had to endorse a product for the ability to give you a refreshing night's slumber then a tyre would now be the last on my list. My neck was really stiff and it took me a few minutes of intense pain to get up. It was then that it dawned on me why the mother always walked around looking like a confused pet pooch. The two eldest children were having an argument as to who was right and who was wrong over something trivial like which was the best chocolate bar. I could see the for and against in each of their points of view as one had caramel and nuts, whilst the other was chewy and had wafers and fruit dispersed throughout.

They were starting to get frustrated with each other so I stepped in to calm them down. I asked for a piece of paper which they were colouring on earlier and wrote the words good on one side and bad on the other. I then made one stand to the left of me, and one stand to the right. Next I asked each child what was written on the paper. Both their answers were different, but they knew they were both correct. It wasn't too long after the exercise and a few scratches on the head that they learnt a valuable lesson that they could take through life, which is just because someone has a different point of view to yours, or has contrasting beliefs it doesn't make them wrong.

The children kept my little diagram and would pull it out when anyone started to argue, much to the annoyance of our leaders, who were the main beneficiaries of the toddlers' constructive talk. I thought how peaceful the world could be in twenty years time if only every child in the world understood the principles of the double-sided page.

POW = Power of Winning

My senses told me that we were making good progress because we had been locked up for over five hours without a stop, had gone over at least a thousands bumps and filled three empty orange coloured bottles! If my bum wasn't tingling and sore from being jostled around then it was feeling numb, and I frequently experienced pins and needles in my legs as well. I could relate to how a hostage would feel and although I knew I'd be released soon, and had the company of four young children, I still suffered small bouts of dejection.

If it wasn't for my creative mind and the ability to visualise I would have probably slumped into a state of deep depression. I decided that a nice sunbathing session on a Jamaican beach was in order, so I got as close to the light as I could, to replicate the sunshine, closed my eyes and started to imagine the waves lapping in, the rays of sunlight shining down and the hot sand beneath me. It was a wonderfully invigorating meditative session, and I genuinely felt that my energy levels had been replenished from it. Prisoners of war that had been locked up for years used the same technique to keep their sanity, and their hope alive. I've heard in documentaries that some of them imagined the most mediocre tasks every day, like taking the bin out or walking round to the shops for the morning paper. The captives that didn't do this, and just accepted their situation are the ones who perished.

The sensuous sights of a topless beach flowing with copious amounts of coconut cocktails vanished in seconds and were replaced with partial darkness when one of the children tapped at my shoulder asked me what it meant. Apparently, in my semi-delirious state I was saying POW over and over again. I thought about the response I should give, as I didn't want it to be negative, and after a few seconds of contemplation asked him what he thought it meant. He huddled with his three brothers like rugby players in a scrum and came out with three words that stunned me.

"Power of Winning?" he said questionably with a shrug of his small, diminutive shoulders.

I was amazed and told him he was spot on, and gave them all a big enthusiastic hug. I suddenly felt that the last few hours in the dark, damp box had probably been the most constructive use of my time ever.

Please Release Me

Despite the magnificent feelings I had been experiencing from the children's new found positivism, I was still relieved when I heard the distinctive hissing sound from the hydraulics, which meant the brakes had been pressed and the convoy had stopped. I put my trainers on, tucked my shirt into my cotton tracksuit bottoms and placed a pair of sunglasses on my head in preparation for the daylight to flood in when the door opened.

Ten minutes later and the latch was still firmly bolted. I was getting restless and the children were biting at the bit to get out. We were all like tied down greyhounds watching a rabbit running into the distance, or bottled up gas itching with energy to let our atoms and molecules loose. Another ten minutes passed and I started banging on the door, followed by shouts, screams and appeals for more bottles, as the ones we had were all full. I could hear clanking in the distance and muffled sounds of activity. Whatever was going on, I wanted to be helping and getting my hands dirty. That was the whole point of being here in the first place, not to sit in a little box but to be helping others in need of assistance, and so far I didn't feel I had achieved anything. The only thing I had left was my vision for the children's home and the knowledge that at least there I'd be leaving something worth while.

The banging finally ceased after thirty minutes and the convoy was rolling again. I couldn't understand why they left us locked up, why the parents didn't want to check on their offspring or why Sharon and James didn't want to rescue me. All sorts of scenarios started to spill over my sound mind. I thought that we could have been hijacked by gangsters, or worse still aliens from another world. After rationalising that our leaders would have bored the Martians back to their own planet or terrorised the terrorists, I then tried to guess exactly what they were up to. I presumed that it was either dodgy or less above board than a windsurfer's tailfin, but never could I ever imagine that they did what they did.

What's the Benefit?

It was another three or four hours before the dusky day light graced the inner sanctum of the God mobile. The metal lined door creaked eerily open and we were greeted by the distinctive setting of yet another motorway service station. I had a mixture of emotions. Part of me was glad to be out in the fresh air with the ability to do simple things that we all take for granted like walk free and pee into something that was larger than an inch across. The other, more discerning side of me was disappointed. I was hoping that the door would be flung open to reveal hundreds of orphans eagerly waiting to help build the best play area that Romania had ever seen. The only children around wanting to build something were the four that I had spent the last six hours with, who jumped over me and bolted out of the door like Gold Cup winning racehorses with one last fence to jump. I didn't have the energy to ask why they kept us locked up for so long because I was too keen to check out the décor at the closest convenience.

I made my way past a man unsuccessfully selling breakdown cover and through the multitude of mobile phone shops. I was desperate to use the toilet but felt compelled to go back and whisper words of encouragement to the unproductive elderly canvasser. He was just sitting on a stool unenthusiastically holding a bland sign that had all the costs involved. I went up to him and shook his hand. He perked up and asked me if I wanted any breakdown cover, but when I told him that I didn't have a car he slumped back onto his chair. I then offered him a two year Harvard Style marketing course in less than two minutes. At first he thought I was being sarcastic but when he could see that I was genuinely concerned he thanked me for taking interest.

I live by the belief that you should help as many people to get on in life as possible even if it means they are going to do better than you because you never know when you might need their help.

My first piece of advice was to dump the stool, stand up proudly and put some energy into the performance. I then asked him the question that would make Saatchi proud, what was the benefit of his service? He told me it was obvious and rolled off a list of advantages. I then told him that it wasn't obvious and instead of selling me a hypothetical black box with buttons he should instead try to motivate me into purchasing a device that will change the channels on my television without the need to get up. He looked at me strangely then mused for a few seconds, before smiling with a glow of inner erudition and finally gave me a warm, hearty hand shake. I made my way to the toilet knowing my good deed for the day was done.

Birch Bojangles Strikes Again

As I stared at the peach-coloured marble tiles and plush advertising boards in front of the automatic flush urinals I felt that something was not quite right. I wasn't sure what it was, but it was like the sensation you get when you're standing outside a girl's house getting ready to take her to a disco, half expecting the blond, blue-eyed bombshell not to be in. I walked out past an arrangement of fresh fragrant fresias and a bowl of pot puree and into the restaurant where everyone was tucking into a vast array of fine foods. Sharon and James were both looking down at their feet avoiding eye contact with me as they munched forlornly on their meal. I thought nothing off it as I went to the serve yourself counter and got myself a small mayonnaise and crouton covered salad and ate it quickly, assuming that they were all just tired. I licked my plate clean and went for a stroll around the shops, past the arcade machines and a crowd of people huddling around the now energetic car recovery specialists to a leaflet stand which was situated just before the exit. There were many handouts for places to visit and boat trips down the Danube, which ruffled every time the automatic sliding doors opened.

My protruding stomach set off the motion sensors on the exit so I thought it would be rude not to go through them. As I walked out into the cold night air there were exhaust fumes billowing from a coach that was about to set off and a tall bearded man stood in front of me. It felt like I was on the set of *Stars in Your Eyes* and I was going to say, "Tonight Matthew, I'm going to be...", when it suddenly dawned on me.

Whenever I have a tingle running down my back and a twitch in my middle finger, it generally means that something is up. I thought about all of the loos I had used in Romania, and none had marble tiles on the wall, let alone fresh flowers. The food was also far superior to anything that I had tasted in the last few weeks and as far as I'm aware, the River Danube doesn't flow through the country I had come to help. It then struck me like a bolt of yellow lightning flashing from the skies. We were in Hungary!

I ran back into the restaurant area and screamed at the group. All the eyes in the room now looked down towards the floor in a blatant act of shame including a couple in the corner who were not even with us. James came over and tried to rationalize saying that he needed to get back to work as quickly as possible. I asked him what we were going to do with all the play equipment for the children, and he tried to put my mind at rest by saying that the vicar who we gave the clothes to had taken it and would make sure it was given to a good home.

I asked James if this was the same vicar that wore lots of jewellery, drove a posh car, lived in a big house and had a gold tooth. James proudly nodded his head as if he'd got a million pound question correct only to shrivel into a shell like protective position when I yelled at the top of my voice, steam once again gushing out of my ears like a clocking off whistle. I had so far given over three weeks of my life, had achieved nothing of significance, helped no one and felt like I had been cheated.

Negative emotions needed to be replaced quickly, and I had to channel my downbeat energy into something positive. All I wanted to do was build a play area for the children and make a difference to their lives and I couldn't do it. I then remembered some inspirational words I read as a young boy that were written in red felt on the back of a toilet door when on a shopping trip to Birmingham with my mum. It read if you want something and you don't get it, then you don't want it. I don't tend to act on things I read on the back of toilet doors in the Midlands, but throughout my years I had made an exception for this piece of life changing advice.

I knew what I wanted to do and no inept, mistrustful and downright dirty couple was going to stand in my way.

The Choice

I was faced with an Andy like choice. Should I grab my bags and head back to Romania to finish the work that I never had chance to start, or do I carry on with the convoy, get home as quickly as possible, never see any of them ever again and organise my own trip. I looked at the two of them, grabbed my bags and started to walk. Then I realised I didn't know which way Romania was, I had no way of getting there and it was starting to rain. I'm never one to let obstacles stand in the way of me achieving my dream, but a little voice inside my head reminded me that I had no play equipment to install when I finally did get back.

The choice was made to get home as promptly as practicable with the team, which would probably be in the blink of an infinite eye.

I wanted to be by myself, and nobody argued when I said that I was going to drive the God mobile. Everyone else scampered into the other vehicles, and the mother and children were shut back into their little cage. I suggested that the two leaders try the box that they were subjecting the family to, but they wouldn't have it and he insisted on driving the old police van, and letting his darling, overweight wife do the map reading. Taz calmed everyone down and we were off down the motorway before any more damaging words could be said. They were taking the lead, and had Taz, James, Sharon and lots of shopping with them. They must have bought a stack of wooden chess boards and sculptures at the boarder because they were pressed up against the back windows and would almost certainly spill out when the back doors had to be opened.

I mulled over to myself how I would have liked to have got a finely chiselled pot, but never had the opportunity. I made it another one of my missions to patronise the pot producers when I went back, and wrote it down in my must do goals list.

I was once again in the cradle with total peace and quiet as no one had the testicular fortitude or audacity to sit alongside me. The only sound I could hear was a slight crackle from a loose connection in the radio and the thumping resonance from every jutting cat's eye that I attempted to flatten. I made sure that the right front wheel to the God mobile crossed over the white line at the side of the road with reckless abandon with all the heartiness of a patriotic flag being waved at rugby final. I was chomping at the bit, waiting for words of condemnation or disapproval to be vented over the CB, but they never came.

Keeping eyeball on me was Geoff and his huge lorry. I looked in my passenger side wing mirror and noticed a flash of ginger hair flowing freely in the wind. I deduced that the Dad must be experiencing the delights of travelling for the first time in the box with the four children, whist the Mum enjoyed the sights and luxury of a real seat, an elevated view of the world and the lavishness of an electric transparent window. I was following the van at a safe distance. I knew that I wasn't too close because I couldn't read their car stickers and the distinctive smell of her off putting underarm odour was now only faint. I always make a point of adhering to the two second rule when driving because I've seen far too many people drive into the back of others, and had it done to me on more than one occasion. I also realised that I didn't want to be too far away as I hadn't got a clue what the right direction was.

A few hours passed at a steady speed and hardly any bends when a large white road sign indicating a new border could be seen in the distance. I was particularly pleased at the progress we had made and frankly felt a flicker of fulfilment at the prospect of being home with friends and family within a few days.

If You're Going to Follow Someone, Make Sure You Know Where They're Going

It only took a droplet of moisture descending from the steamed up window to extinguish my delightful flicker. That and a six foot sign that welcomed us to Yugoslavia! This meant that for the last nine hours, not only had we not been making progress, but had actually been going back. We would have made far more advancement if we had spent the whole day drinking coffee and not moved at all.

In every part of my life, from hobbies to work to home, I always find someone to follow, a person to emulate whom I respect and admire. If they are where I want to be in life, then that's who I model myself on. If you want to be a great footballer, then there is no point in taking advice from an architect and if you want to design magnificent buildings, then David Beckham is not your man. But the other way round you have yourself a dream team combination.

Following the two of them for the last 400 miles was as bad as if not worse than wanting to be famous and listening to and taking advice from a refuse collector. Through the stickered up window and past the many various wooden objects, luggage and souvenirs I could clearly see a selection of silhouetted arms waving about aggressively followed by the familiar fumes of burning rubber pooled with the sound of the screeching brakes.

The two got out waving their fingers in the air and looked for someone to blame. Geoff was the first target for not telling them they were going the wrong way, and then they started on Taz for messing around with the map. When the tears started to flow, they then looked in my direction, but a frosty stare from me put a seal on any incumbent accusations. I never expected them to take responsibility for their actions and their behaviour was true to their frighteningly foreseeable form. The wrangling was halted by a barely audible, muffled gurgle. At first I thought it was my stomach yearning for some protein, but it was the Dad, who was kicking and punching at the door to the God mobile, begging to be let out. I knew what it felt like and bearing no malice, went over to the well-latched door and let him out.

I don't think I've ever seen a sight quite like it. He really looked as though he was death warmed up, with a greenish, yellow complexion and frothing at the mouth. He staggered out with all the strength and finesse of a fly carrying an elephant on its back. I was showing him real concern and compassion, and was honestly worried for his well-being, but when he told me that he started feeling nauseous after he drank some flat fizzy orange I couldn't help myself and burst out in a fit of uncontrolled laughter. No one else understood the joke, except for the children who were holding back their giggles and the group looked at me quizzically as though I'd just blasphemed in church on Easter Sunday. There was the Dad, green at the gills while I was almost splitting my sides.

I was sure there was knowledge to be gained from this escapade and after lots of thought and deliberation, decided that the message was to learn from other people's mistakes. That is called wisdom and I can honestly say that as a result of that fateful day I have never ever drunk freshly squeezed urine, not knowingly anyway!

After a game of domino vomiting, when one starts and everyone else joins in, it was decided to make the most of a bad situation and take in a few local sights. We drove straight through the border and travelled for about a mile. A cracked bricked wall and a footbridge later and we turned around to leave the country that we had no intention of entering in the first place.

For no apparent reason the seemingly quiet road had transformed into a bustling highway, and there was a long winding tailback at the border. I could foresee another long delay and after four hours of queuing, eight hours of interrogation and a strip search of the van, my psychic abilities had not lost their credibility. I pride myself on doing things that normal people don't even think about, let alone try, and I was minutes away from adding yet another first to my long list of uncommon accomplishments.

After leaving Yugoslavia for what I hoped was the last time in my life I was mentally preparing myself for this inaugural experience. This one, despite being exceptional was not one that I would relish boasting about; it wasn't white-water rafting or anything that could be considered exhilarating. I wouldn't even lose my breath and break out into a sweat pulling off the feat; it was crossing the Hungarian boarder for the fifth time in less than three weeks.

Take the Straight Road

If you want to get on in life then there is one piece of advice that you should always take into consideration. Firstly know where you want to go and then find the quickest route possible. It really is that simple, but the majority of people make it complicated by procrastinating or putting their dreams aside for more important things like watching the television!

After reluctantly relenting from Romania for the last time on the trip I knew where it was that I wanted to go, and that was home. Unfortunately for me, I was not in total control of my destiny and the dysfunctional drove was intent on making life difficult. If I had been plotting the route, which would have been researched scrupulously, there would have been a nice straight line with the occasional twist or turn to allow for hills and streams. Our navigational leaders chose not to do any research, and their map looked like the work of a child with a nervous twitch who had slipped whilst using a Spiro graph.

We spent the rest of the day going round in circles and even saw signs for Romania. A few more left turns and some invaluable advice from Geoff and we were back on track.

How many people fritter their lives going round and round in circle, squandering forty years travelling from home to work, work to home day after day not knowing that there is a better life available for them? If they only broke the monotony of their predictable sequence, wrote on paper exactly where they wanted to go with a date they wanted to be there and followed it through like a straight line on a map, then their lives would be filled with much more meaning.

Sharon and James came up to me and asked if we could travel together as a threesome in the God mobile. James suggested that as there was no leadership. Together we would be stronger and head the convoy. They both apologised for letting me down, knowing how dearly I wanted to build the playground but they had gone through all they could take from the trip and wanted to get home without delay. I never hold any malice towards anyone no matter what they've done to me because I quite enjoy the feeling of inner peace, so I swung open the door and welcomed them in.

I told them how I, as a well-focused forward thinking individual was frustrated at constantly going the wrong way and how it equated to a mediocre man lacking direction. They both simultaneously slumped. I asked what was wrong and James said he had been an accountant for years and was bored, and hoped this would kick-start a new life. Sharon also explained how her job lacked the edge she was looking for, and although she wanted to remain in the caring profession, desired something fresh and new. They seemed to perk up when I complimented them for knowing what they didn't want because that is just as important as knowing what you do want. I then encouraged them to write their ideal dream down on a piece of paper and keep it safe.

I reached into my pocket and pulled out a newspaper cutting, which was dated the third and tore it into two. Sharon tore her piece in half again and encouraged me to do the same. I said that all my goals were all ready down, but if I put a new one on the shred she gave me we could all match the pieces together like a jigsaw puzzle in a year's time when they had all come to fruition. The three of us pondered for a few minutes and started to scribe, before folding the papers up safely. I had no idea at that moment what they did pen onto those small scraps, but I knew what mine was and looked forward to the possibility of renovating that page, dated the third back to its former glory with sticky tape. We all nodded at each other knowing that the future was now in our hands and the only person from stopping us achieving what was written down was the person that had written it.

Everyone Wants to Be a Leader, but Only a Few Can Lead

We made great progress at the head of the convoy, and travelled nearly a thousand miles in the right direction, which was more of a novelty than not having socks for Christmas. As France got ever closer, we were overtaken by the two in the van. They swerved past us like a crazed gorilla that had devoured one too many bananas and promptly switched their hazard lights on. We all stopped on the side of the road and waited to find out what was wrong. Nothing happened for a few minutes so I got out from behind my wheel and walked towards them. As I got closer, I noticed him pick his mobile phone up and start to have an imaginary conversation. You can always tell when someone is doing this because they exaggerate their nonverbal communication and the head movements are never in sync with the words. You can even tell if a trained Shakespearian actor is having a real exchange or not by the way he nods his head.

I knocked on the window and he kept me waiting for a few seconds before nodding frantically into the handset like a novelty dog in the back of a car. He finally put the phone down and said he'd just been told that we had to pick up an urgent aid package to take back to the U.K. from somewhere on the outskirts of Paris, and it was fine because he had booked the ferry and it was not leaving until first thing in the morning. I knew something was slightly strange. Firstly, I couldn't believe he'd be so organised as to actually forward plan, and secondly, the U.K. was not in dire need of any imperative aid. We certainly didn't have any volcanoes exploding and as far as I was aware there had not been a drought in the last three weeks.

He also said that I had taken the convoy the long route and if he had been leading the way like he should have been, we would have made the trip in half the time! I wasn't going to rise to the occasion. Throughout my life I've been associated with different individuals who get a kick out of making other people's days bad, just to make themselves feel better or more important, and I wasn't going to let him spoil mine. Instead of biting back I calmly walked with confidence to the God mobile and wrote down ten top tips for being a successful leader. These included gems such as never criticise the people you work with in public, save it for a private place if it really is warranted and always take responsibility for your actions.

I finished writing down the tenth top tip, which babies cry for and soldiers die for, and that's to motivate your team with positive recognition. This can be as simple as saying well done or a plain pat on the back. I then neatly folded the sheet in half and walked back over to the van and asked if we could have a moment's privacy. He hesitantly agreed and as all good leaders do I took him to the side where no one else could hear and coolly said that his actions were not appropriate. I then presented him with the top tips as a gesture of goodwill. He looked at it, laughed, ripped it into pieces, tossed it over his shoulder and walked away ridiculing me to everyone else. Now that's great leadership!

The whole team was now at it's most negative state, and if I could have pooled a vote of no confidence then I would have, but he vaulted into his van and started to drive away before we had chance to call for a motion. Geoff was subsequently ensuing and I had to drive the rest of the team as well. It's not that I'm a follower, because I'm not. I'm the sort of person who orders a double helping of sorbet when everyone else has plumped for the apple pie, but I had the team to think about and there is no I in team.

Scenic Tour of France

When I agreed to do an aid mission to Romania I had no idea, not the slightest inclination, that the Eiffel Tower would be on the sightseeing list but that's exactly where he had to do his meet and greet, despite telling us it was on the outskirts of the city.

We all waited in the van as we were eager to get going, and finally be on the water with home just a stone's throw away. I should have guessed it wouldn't be the easiest thing in the world as he took more than two hours to complete whatever business he had to do and came back with expensive looking designer bags overflowing with shopping and a strange-shaped item wrapped in bin liners.

Out of one of the bags came a bright metallic yellow-coloured car sticker that changed when you moved it, which he proudly fixed to the back windscreen ensuring even less light could penetrate the inside of the van. He also got out a packet of blue-tac, tore off a generous chunk and rolled it into a ball. I thought this might be a new type of Chinese stress reliever, but it wasn't to be. He slapped the rolled up fixer onto his dashboard just to the side of the porcelain horse and took out a cheap-looking model of the Arc de Triumph. The grand structure was now pride of place in the van, surrounded by fairy lights and plastic clowns. He spent a few minutes making sure it was balanced but by the time he finished it was still wonky. It looked more like the Leaning Tower of Pisa than a fine French architectural feature.

For the first time in my experience he appeared to be focussed. The look of a hungry tiger was evident in his eyes and he seemed to have direction. Unfortunately, it wasn't fixed at the remainder of the trip just where to conceal his weird-shaped parcel. He took the mysterious item and placed it in the back of the God mobile, the lorry that I was driving. I was perplexed as to why he didn't put it in his own vehicle and also slightly concerned.

I've been on many trips abroad and the first thing that customs ask you, even if you're just carrying a bag, is if you packed it yourself. I thought about trying to explain what a two foot tall giraffe wrapped up in black plastic was doing in an otherwise empty van. I then wondered why the said item would be considered in any way medical aid and was it worth the large detour?

I told him that I wasn't happy carrying it as I didn't know what it was, and there was plenty of room next to the other anomalous items he had been given by the man with gold teeth. He said that it was just a toy he had won in the fair whilst standing next to a poster promoting the carnival which finished a week ago. I pointed at the sign. He went bright red and stomped over to the back of the God mobile, picked up the strange item, which had a powdery rattle and hid it under a pile of wooden pots and luggage at the back of his old van. Considering it was just a toy, he did his best to conceal it and I doubted its legitimacy. Maybe it was a counterfeit toy! He then changed the subject away from the contents of his parcel and the distinct lack of any medical aid and suggested we go or we might miss the boat. Everyone agreed and scampered into the lorries that Geoff and I were driving, leaving just the two of them in the van with a stuffed Giraffe for company.

Character Building

Geoff put his foot down and took the lead, followed closely by the ever-glowing, very rusty God mobile and the two of them trailing behind. Sharon, James and Taz were squeezed into the front besides me but nobody complained, not about the lack of room anyway. We all talked about how the trip was nearing an end and agreed that despite not achieving any of the goals that we set out to accomplish, we were still richer from the experience. Taz said that she had missed her family whilst she was away and realised that they weren't as bad as she had previously thought. She was looking forward to getting on with her mum and doing simple mother/daughter like pleasures like going shopping together.

James and Sharon were clutching their pieces of paper. They really didn't know which way their life was going to flow before the trip but now they had a course to follow. They both understood that the saying, "If it's to be, then it's up to me," was true and that they shouldn't just dream of their ideal life, but live the dream.

I said that it had been character building. I now knew what made for a good leader, and just as importantly what made for a bad one. I certainly understood how not to behave to get ahead and influence others. I had matured into a better person and developed a level head. If you're in a negative situation, like a job you don't like, then change it, but use your time there to build on and enhance your character. Become stronger from your experiences and learn from it.

It was agreed by all that the trip had not been a waste of energy, but a pivotal time in our lives and that realization made the rest of the journey to the docks much more pleasant.

Geoff got us to the harbour with great efficiency and the sights and smells of the fresh sea air were exhilarating, but not as fantastic as seeing the awesome English ferry berth with ballet-like grace to the quay-side. From our vantage point we could see the vast selection of left and right wheeled cars, lorries and people disembark. When the vessel was empty I got ready to board, making sure my passport was to hand and that all documentation was ready to be displayed. Finally the trip was nearly over. Or was it?

He came running out of the terminal building shouting obscenities aimed at our French friends combined with innuendoes, which included inserting sharp pointed objects up the anal passage of toad-like creatures. I was not in the least surprised that something was amiss, but questioned what it was.

Apparently, despite being told the crossing was booked, we wouldn't be able to get onto a ship for four days because they were all full. For the hundredth time on the trip a positive mood changed instantly to scenes of near riot like chaos. I calmed the situation down with my recently acquired leadership skills and level headedness and pondered on the situation.

I noticed two French drivers arguing to each other about a broken down lorry with a cargo of fruit that needed urgent delivery. I told them that my friend had a spare lorry and was free for a few days and then went and told Geoff about the challenge. Within an hour they had transferred the load and our flat cap wearing Yorkshire man was happily honking his horn a few thousand pounds the richer. There was still the challenge of the rest of the group either spending another three days away from home, or coming up with a solution. It's not customary for a bag of passing air to be the answer to your predicament, but this floating elucidation drifted by as a ray of sunlight filled the sky and a rainbow formed in front of us. I suggested that those who didn't have to drive catch a passenger hovercraft.

The gruesome twosome started disagreeing and saying how it would be best to stay together, especially with the threat of piracy at an all time high. Before I had chance to laugh I hopped over to the booking in department to see if there were any vacancies on the hovercraft. Ten places were available on the next ferry which was leaving in ten minutes. I booked the tickets, ran back and gave the good news. We all grabbed our belongings, including the two of them who were caught up in the emotion, and started to head for the crafts launching pad. They then stopped dead in their tracks as it dawned on them it was just for passengers, and didn't include the two vehicles. As they scratched their heads I threw the keys to the God mobile at him and wished them both sincerely the best of luck as we skipped without them to the waiting hovercraft.

As we were joyfully embarking into the ultra modern vessel his parting words, which were nearly drowned out by the noise of the starting fans were, "Who's up for the next mission?"

Twelve Months on...

It's been a year since I got back, and in that time I've set up a successful fair trade company selling Romanian wooden pots. The men who make them get paid a decent amount for each one, far greater than they were ever getting before, and I sell them back in the U.K. to a major department store.

All of the profits go to training Romanian children in IT and internet skills. I've also sold designer sixties furniture to a posh shop in Fulham, and all the money from that has paid for a state of the art medical facility complete with a new shower block and toilet at the tuberculosis hospital where Sharon now works, and she currently has a gold ring on her finger. She got engaged in March to the head doctor, and they're both very happy.

I've also designed my playground, and it proudly stands in the grounds of the children's home in Brazov, and Geoff, who helped me take it over, is now married to one of the nurses and helps to look after the kids.

James has quit his job as an accountant and at present offers relaxing massages for a very reasonable price, and also collects old mobile phones for use by the Romanian ambulance service.

The three of us, Sharon, James and I, were invited to the Mayor of Brazov's office a short time ago, and were awarded freedom of the city for services rendered. The front page of the local newspaper had a big bold headline which read "The Extraordinary Three"and included a cheesy photo of us surrounded by children.

In my new office, just behind a large oak desk I have a frame hanging on the wall. In it are three scraps of newspaper which are held together by sticky tape. Each of the pieces has different writing on them, but the same date, the third, exactly a year from when they were written.

Run of the mill people may have just accepted what they were dished out, and passed the trip off as a bad learning experience, but we made the conscious decision that we wanted to make a positive difference and leave a legacy. We could only do that by giving that bit extra and not putting up with second best.

I don't know what the two are up to now, but I'm sure they're stringing others along. I just hope that they, too, will be able to learn life changing lessons from their experiences, as we did.

The highlight of it all, the thing that really makes life worth living is the end result from the simple dream building session twelve months before. If Sharon had not tore off a piece of paper and encouraged me to write at that specific time then I would have never printed the name Gabby. It was just on my mind at that time. It now hangs on my wall, behind my desk, on newspaper in a frame.

It took me months to find her, but I had a date down and a dream, and I could not let my goal go by without trying. Life is now wonderful with my gorgeous angelic dark-hared girlfriend with the soft, gentle touch and a cute accent, and boy, does she look great in black!

The End

Printed in the United Kingdom
by Lightning Source UK Ltd.
100871UKS00003B/577-672